Humming
in Spanish

Books by Ginna BB Gordon

The Soup Kit
  A comprehensive map for creating good soups from scratch

The Lavandula Series
  Based on the fictional journals of Stefani Michel
  Book One: *Looking for John Steinbeck*
  Book Two: *Deke Interrupted*
  Book Three: *Humming in Spanish*

The Honey Baby Darlin' Series
  A serial memoir about cooking, love, & the love of cooking
  Book One: *Bonnebrook*
  Book Two: *The Gingerbread Farm*

Sunny Mae & Bird in Alaska
  A read-aloud book with illustrations by Dai Thomas

First You Grow the Pumpkin
  100 Cool Things to Make and Preserve

The Marriage Tip Book
  Advice from the Wise Ones of the 2nd Grade
    with Nan Heflin

A Simple Celebration
  The Nutritional Program from
  the Chopra Center for Well Being
   as Ginna Bell Bragg, with David Simon, MD
   Foreword by Deepak Chopra (pub. by Random House)

Visit www.luckyvalleypress.com

Humming in Spanish

Book Three in *The Lavandula Series*

Based on the fictional journals
of Stefani Michel

Ginna BB Gordon

Tiny Paintings by
Dai Thomas

Lucky Valley Press
2021

Humming in Spanish

© 2021 Ginna BB Gordon

All Rights Reserved

Book Three in The Lavandula Series

ISBN: 978-0-578-67264-9

Sweet Farm illustrations by the author

Tiny Paintings based on originals by Dai Thomas

Cover art by Melissa Lofton, acrylic on wood *(detail)*

Produced and Published in 2021
by Lucky Valley Press
Jacksonville, Oregon
www.luckyvalleypress.com

*[Cannery Row's] inhabitants are, as the man once said,
"whores, pimps, gamblers, and sons of bitches," by which
he meant everybody. Had the man looked through another
peephole he might have said, "saints and angels and martyrs
and holy men," and he would have meant the same thing.*
– John Steinbeck
Cannery Row

The best worlds are built on good connections.
– Ginna BB Gordon

It's all about relationships.
– Marc Allen

Cast of Characters with ages in 1964

Jock "Poppy" Wyman, *Patriarch*   80

Maria "Mama Maria" Wyman, *Matriarch*   70

Their Daughters

   Rita Grace Wyman Michel   40

   Nancy "Nana" Wyman Huffington   37

   Nora "Fox" Wyman Harley   35

The Cousins

   Stefani "Stevie" Awena Michel *(Rita's daughter)* 15

   Jolene Huffington *(Nana's daughter)*   15

   Tate Marie Wyman *(Fox's daughter)*   16

Husbands/BFs

   Stefáno "Fáno" Michel   45
   (Rita's husband, father of Stevie)

   Charles "Chuck" Huffington   43
   (Nana's husband, father of Jolene, deceased)

   Deke Harley   40
   (Fox's no longer missing partner, father of Tate)

Prologue

Tate Wyman says:

When my father, Deke Harley, disappeared in 1950, I was 2 and a half years old. All I remembered was his scent. The slightest hint of English Leather made me cry. My childhood music teacher, Mr. Dzuro, was English Leathered. I couldn't breathe sitting next to him at the piano.

And I remembered what I called my dad: De. I remembered that when I was restless in the night, he took me outside with a blankie and pillow to look at stars. For a few years I conjured up the sound of his voice, a kind of murmur in the dark of night, and his fingers, pointing to the sky. But then I lost that, too. So, when he came home, I didn't know him at all. All I cared about was that he was home. He still smelled like English Leather.

My mother longed for him (secretly, she imagined) for 13 years with a quiet ferocity with which I couldn't compete. And then, he came home…all changed. She had missed a kind of static Deke Harley, the mythical James Dean twin, the soul-surrendering sizzling love affair. She didn't relate one little bit to this new guy who called himself Deke Harley, couldn't get past the "half a brain," as he put it, and the injury that altered his life so swift and sure. Oh, I know these things now, and I understand my mother more as I get older. But I didn't care that she wasn't all gaga and gooey-eyed over his return. He was my dad, and he was home.

And it was good. But, then everything got muddled up even more. That's when I crawled into a tiny hole and curled up in a ball. Thank God for music, it saved my life. I wrote dark songs with titles like Drown my Sorrow in the Moonlight and Prom Only Means the End of Wonder. I was dramatic, but I hurt inside.

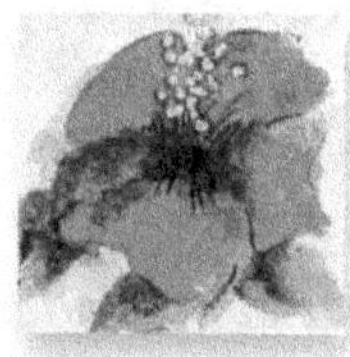 **Jo Huff says:**

My dad was dead. No disrespect to Tate's problems, but there was no bringing my father back. He was gone, and what was left to my mother and me was a mystery to unravel, like a basket of loose entangled yarn. It would take the two of us to gently hold the yarn and ease it apart, loop by loop. At this point, we weren't doing much of a job of it. We argued a lot.

When I let go of the imaginary box at the beach in Big Sur the year before, I expunged the guilt for letting my father drive away from Sweet Farm the night he died, but he didn't leave my side, oh no. He hummed in my ear, still, which made me twitch and gave me the feeling we weren't finished—that he had more to say. I was happy to bide my time and go back to school and let him rest. Nana, my mother, was chomping at the bit to unravel the story, but she had ulterior motives.

So my memory of 1964 is a jumble.

You'll see here, thanks to Stevie's excellent journals and a memory like a library card file, that my dad didn't so much die as take on invisibility. You'll think I'm crazy, and maybe I am, but if I'm whacked, so was my mum, because she heard his voice, too. He followed us around, like he was right behind us, wearing his London Fog coat with the belt hanging low on one side. I could see him in my peripheral vision, but when I turned my head, he vanished.

 **Stevie says:**

L isten, and I'll try to make sense of the story.

About Stevie

Stefani Awena Michel was born at home in the Chapel House on Sweet Farm, in her own room, as it turned out, on a rainy Thursday night in late September, 1948. Rita did not plan to have this baby at home (hospital births being more popular at the time). Stefani, anxious to get on with it, had other ideas and slithered into the arms of her surprised father, Fáno, just after midnight on the 30th.

Rita and Fáno had positioned the last two items of baby furniture in the new room. The Chapel House was barely livable (unpainted walls, unfinished floors) but Rita wanted to be in her own home by the time her baby was born. Well, that worked out.

Her water broke about 11:30 pm while she fitted the little flannel sheet to the crib mattress. She laid herself down on the single bed in the corner while Juana, friend and fellow compound resident, went off to find Jock for the ride to Community Hospital. Jock, Rita's father, patriarch of Sweet Farm, was the owner and driver of the only vehicle on the farm at the time.

Ten minutes later Juana returned and found Fáno sitting on the edge of the little bed holding his slimy baby girl in her birthday suit, still attached by a thin little cord to her beaming and laughing mother. Rita took the scissors from the side table and reached over her deflated tummy to cut the cord. Fáno wrapped the baby in a little blanket and gave her back to Rita, by then scooched up on the pillows with her dress down and her arms out. Juana handed Rita a wet cloth, so she wiped the little baby's face and pressed her to her breast.

From the time she spoke her first word, "book," Stefani Awena Michel was the first up in the morning, the last to go to sleep and in between, always, as her mother pointed out, "into something."

"Book!" she'd cry! This brought her mother to the bed to read a bedtime story, every night.

Stevie was born under the Libra sign of the Zodiac: "a natural peacemaker, an expert at tactful and diplomatic relationships with a strong sense of justice."

To a T.

Stevie tried like crazy to look on the bright side of everything, but she found it difficult, people being so silly and all. As one of a large family, the Wymans (most of whom lived at least part time on Sweet Farm) there were plenty of opportunities for observation.

In both the formal Honors English Journals and her private Little Red Books, as she discovered and wrote about the world around her, Stevie chronicled the Wyman sisters, their daughters and the men involved. It's a rich, colorful tapestry, sewn together by threads of stories.

Part One

Chapter One

January-March 1964
Sweet Farm
Carmel Valley California

New Year's R.E.S.O.L.U.T.I.O.N.S.

#1
Remember you are 15.
It is a very in-between age, not a child, not an adult. Mid.
Confusing at best. Don't screw it up by acting like you are 25.
You do not think like a 25 year old.

#2
Think longer and harder before you act.
The choices you make today will follow you around for the
rest of your life. Don't be stupid. See above.

#3
STOP this fixation on lips. Kissing is out of the question.

#4

Keep a tether on your imagination, at least in your personal life. It only gets you in trouble. Save it for writing or for your abstract painting class.

#5

Aspire to be like Mama Maria and Sister William. Why. Because both women at least appear to be calm and creative without the drama, unlike both aunts, or yourself. [I want to be like my mother, but she is perfect, so I shall never attain her likeness. She is not human. She is actually an elf or faerie or maybe even a true angel. She has every attribute but the wings].

#6

Be a better cousin and friend.

You were so wrapped up in your own little self-inflicted tragic-comedy that you did not show enough interest in Tate's most extraordinary and real-life regaining of her father. Get over that other thing. Get over IT.

#7

In terms of getting over IT, you made it all up in the first place, so you can unmake it. Do that. Do it methodically, like unraveling a sweater so you can make it into something else.

#8

So, you're going to be a writer. Be a writer, instead of a nitwit. (See above.)

Stevie's Sweet Farm home sits on a flat ten acre parcel in mid Carmel Valley, known as Mid Valley. Sweet Farm's backyard is the Carmel River. Well, its backyard is actually six acres of lavender plants, about 15,000 this year, Fáno calculated. But the river is back there, burbling away. The other side of the river is a gateway to Los Padres National Forest.

Culinary herbs proliferate on Sweet Farm, too: basil and oregano and rosemary. Thyme pops up between the sand-stone pavers, Echinacea lines the paths. Flowers and bushes as well as greens, beans, tomatoes, cucumbers, apricot, peach and pear trees and myriad vines meander through-out the property. It spreads around the Barn, along the slat fence of the Rodriguezes' cottage, up to and into the walled yard around Jock and Maria's Adobe House. It floats along the walkway to the Chapel House, where Stevie lives with her parents.

To get to Sweet Farm from Highway 1, it's a quick Carmel Valley Road journey, east toward the sunrise (away from the coast) about four miles. In the time of our story, Mid Valley is a sleepy little community in Monterey County—not part of tourist-y famous Carmel-by-the-Sea, not in country-style Carmel Valley Village, but in between. Mid. It is rural, lush in winter, golden in summer, productive in husbandry, with local dairies and farm stands and co-ops, horses and stables, children on horseback or bicycles, tractors in wide open fields.

When the Wymans bought the farm in 1940, all that remained of the MacIntoshes' 40 acre orchard were 10 flat acres, a few scruffy buildings and three ancient pear trees, which surprised all by sprouting and blossoming the next spring. By that fall, Jock and Maria and their teen-aged daughters, Rita, Nana and Fox, with sticky sweet pear juice dribbling down their chins, christened their new home Sweet Farm.

Fáno Michel felt the spirits of the Esselen and Rumsen Indians in Los Padres. Ever since his arrival at Sweet Farm back in 1948, he felt at home. It was a good feeling. His French Romani soul resonated with the sacred lands, the tribal secrets, the vividness of the shades of green.

It is a fertile land, abundant of crops and sweet of fruit. When Fáno tended the plants, most days he stepped into a native feeling, as if he were hundreds of years old, caring for this land for eons. It was his mother's blood coursing through that connected him to these ancient peoples, but also, a universal feeling of loving and protecting the land, guardian to the soul of it, the life of it.

The mountains (hills, really), the walls of Carmel Valley vary in colors throughout the year. In spring come Lupin and California poppies, blankets of blues and oranges deep and layered with color. It makes your heart pine for something, but you just can't put your finger on it. A sweet heartache of beauty. Ice plant like Purple Carpet takes over and then throughout the summer, the hills go through greens from sea foam and seaweed to olive, emerald, lime and chartreuse to yellow and then to gold. And, of course, the wild flowers!

When Deke Harley re-appeared out of nowhere on the Sweet Farm doorstep just before the previous Thanksgiving, it was a sunny 65.° Apples were falling from the trees, tomatoes still ripened on the vines and late cabbages curled their leaves in the garden. All the doors of the Sweet Farm buildings were wide open, breezes wafted through with aromas from the Tea Room as well as the Distillery, a steamy lavender essence merging with brown sugar and yeast.

Now, in January, Stevie's sliding door is cracked open a bare three inches, to hear the sound of the rain while she writes. It's cold and wet. Her little desk faces east, the window usually offering a glorious view of the sun rising over Sweet Farm. It dapples the trees, glows on the rooftops, and tips the leaves of every plant.

Today, the sky is still dark at 7am, the heavy rain droning since dawn. The splash of rain drops on the deck roused Stevie early, eager as she was to begin the New Year, with new eyes, new R.E.S.O.L.U.T.I.O.N.S. She tiptoed out to the kitchen, brewed a cup of English Breakfast Tea and toasted an English Muffin. She was not ready for a PB&J. She might never eat peanut butter again.

The resolutions came fast and furious. She could barely keep up with the things she wanted to change. She didn't know there could be so many at the tender age of 15.

Stevie is not quite 5 foot 2 inches tall, and from behind one might think she is a child and not 15 going on 30. Her behind is a bit flat and she has no hips to speak of, not yet, though her true womanhood is beginning to round out.

Stevie's ropey braid hangs down her back almost to the waist. It is black hair, thick and coarse. In certain fits of pique, Stevie threatens to cut it off but chickens out when the scissors are near. The hairs on her arms stand up and vibrate with shared enthusiasm, like a crowd protest to save the braid.

Stevie isn't beautiful by 60s American standards. Her structure is compact, her face peasant soft, with the high cheekbones and latte skin of her father's nomadic people. Stevie's gray Frida Kahlo eyes, fringed with dark lashes and heavy brows, miss nothing. The eyes glitter with tiny gold flecks, little mirrors gathering light. She watches the world, wary, ready to pounce or retreat, depending. There is a grace to her movements that compels one to look again, a panther moving across the land.

She has little fear, too little, really, as she discovered last fall, but still she misses no opportunity to focus those gray eyes on the next person or event. Stevie Michel has a cataloging kind of mind, with files, some on paper, some in her head, for valuable quotes, conversations, colors, causes, outfits, antics, even recipes, though she's not the most dedicated cook.

The girl was born in jeans and a t-shirt. Upon her sudden awareness of James Dean at the age of ten (he died on her birthday, when she was an innocent seven), she "borrowed" a few white t-shirts from her father, Fáno's, closet. He'd never miss them, being more of a paisley guy. She rolled up her sleeves and tucked the white t-shirt into jeans and that was that. Her closet became so simple—Santa Lucia uniform weekdays, T shirts and jeans forever else. The opposite of her half-British cousin, Jolene, who exchanged her Woolsley School uniform for fashion, as often as possible, the kookier the better.

Stevie liked to curl up in a chair and become invisible and yet when she walked down the street, she turned heads. Of this, she was completely clueless, which was part of her charm.

This is not to say she was unaware of the opposite sex. Au contraire! She was aware, and anxious.

Last fall she had a perfect plan. When the plan went awry, she lost her courage. She imploded, a little; deflated, dejected, disappointed in herself.

Stevie's Little Red Book
The Wedding

Fox and Deke were married today, January 5, 1964.

Fox's "keep it simple" rule was firm. We turned Christmas decorations into winter wedding décor. My mother, Rita, made a three layered carrot cake with cream cheese frosting. No guests came to the wedding, just us, the family. And Father Green, who performed the Episcopal ceremony, and the Rodriguezes, official witnesses. (Ha. Seriously, since 1945. They are family.)

Out of eight women on the Sweet Farm compound, not one wore a dress for the occasion. Not even the bride. Her crisp white shirt was a simple homage to the sacredness of a wedding, but her jeans and boots were ubiquitous (my word of the week). Only Mama Maria wore a skirt, one of those long, button-down-the-front jobs she loves so much. She dressed herself up with a jaunty scarf, pinned to the side with a cameo brooch.

In typical me-style, I spent most of my time evaluating the quality and differences in everyone's jeans. Jeans tell you volumes. It's ironic that only Deke's jeans were pressed. Mine have a hole in the knee. Poppy's were rolled up above his white socks and Jo Huff's were black velvet, covered in Guatemalan embroidery. And, of course, my father's jeans have calico patch pockets.

16

My other cousin (jeans made distinctive by the glitzy belt) is happy. And, why wouldn't she be? Her father has come home, alive and mostly well, her parents have finally gotten married after sixteen years and, as Tate says, she is "no longer a bastard."

Aunt Fox tried to convince herself and the rest of us that this wedding was a practical matter for Tate and her comfort, but I can only imagine what has gone on inside Aunt Fox's mind during the week preparing for it. Not practical things, for sure. She, of course, doesn't talk to anyone about her feelings, so who knows? Maybe her sisters, my mother and Aunt Nana, have a clue, but I doubt it.

She just doesn't look happy...she looks...determined: determined to be nice to Deke, to pretend everything is fine, to give Tate what she wants. Resolute also comes to mind. But all in all, she looks like a cornered animal.

She always looks like a cornered animal. A fox, I suppose.

She and Deke have gone to the little cottage in Ben Lomond for a few days honeymoon. I'd like to be a fly on that wall.

Tate and I go back to Lucia on Wednesday, the day Jo and Aunt Nana return to London.

We are all ready for some kind of normal. Deke shows up after thirteen years in November. Two months later, he and Fox are married and about to live together again in the Barn apartment. Two months! How did she do it?

January 7, 1964
Water Under the Bridge

Three girls munched tuna sandwiches and shared a thermos of tea. At 50° and a little windy, they were bundled up and protected by the bridge pillars. Stevie's fingerless gloves came in handy, as did the miles of hand knit scarves, their abundant Lavandula Studio creations.

This, then, was the last Girl Cousins Club get together before Jo left for London and they all went back to school.

Jo said, "So what happens now, Tate? I mean, Deke's only been here since November and now, all of a sudden, poof! Married!"

"I know. It's fast. But it does change things, in a good way, don't you think? Maybe we can settle down now? Just sort of live our lives? You know, really live, like, we're not waiting for something to happen or for the other shoe to drop."

"Ha!" said Stevie. "Do you think everyone will suddenly pretend thirteen years never happened?"

"No, no, not that. I mean, it's amazing and wonderful and, frankly, pretty weird for me but, it's not what my mother wants. But, no one knows what she wants. She's just doing it to make me happy. I'd just like a few years of something more normal. I'm tired of wondering what ifs and whys, you know? Feelings of loss but not knowing what I'd lost."

Jo says, "It really is weird, Tate. I mean, we thought your dad was dead and here he is back again and my dad is really, truly dead, but keeps showing up, like some apparition or ghost. Crikey, just when I thought things were better, it gets even more complicated. My mum doesn't believe the curse story, you know, so…"

Stevie wandered into her interior landscape while the other cousins contemplated their fathers; one dead, one back from the presumed dead.

Whenever Tate mentioned her dad, Stevie stepped out of the conversation, like backing off from a barking dog. Her Deke secret had flags all over it and she was afraid they were red and waving and calling out for notice. She tried to make the flags invisible, but when she was with Jo or Tate, or both, that didn't work well. She felt vulnerable, transparent. *Someday it all will be revealed*, she thought.

So far, they didn't seem to notice her shift in presence, wrapped up as they were in their father dramas. Stevie squirmed on the rock and looked at something shiny on the beach.

Human and nature's debris washed up on the small beaches of the Carmel River. The young cousins liked to hang out on the Rock under the Schulte Road Bridge and watch for critters, discuss the greatness and the silliness of the universe, discover driftwood, tumbled rocks, bottle caps, bottles, flakes of river mica.

Bobcats cruise the river for moles, voles, ground squirrels and water. They rustle through high weeds and grasses while frogs belch, birds sing and crickets rub white sound on tiny violin legs. The occasional bear dips her snout in (although the cousins have never seen one, they know she's there). The deer and raccoons and smaller fury things that dare, nose around the narrow weedy path. Mountain lions hunt all. The girls have their Fáno-carved sticks, just in case.

All Wymans eventually spent time on Charles Wayland Huffington's Rock under the Schulte Road Bridge, remembering his poem, the one that took them by surprise, since everyone looked at the young Lord Charles as a lost and hopeless drunk, not a dreaming, sad, articulate poet. They would remember him or think about their own lives. It was their Rock, the cousins painted CWH on it in white, they did not forget him. No one stashed a flask of gin in the bushes, a la Chuck; just as well.

Chuck's poem was etched in their minds, but here's a reminder, in case you've forgotten Charles Huffington and his favorite place (a big flat rock under the Schulte Road Bridge) and where he took his final breath (under the Bixby Bridge in Big Sur).

My Peaceful Willows

This rock is where I find my peace
The bridge protects me from all eyes
The willows are my tender friends
The moon shines in the starry skies

I have no teddy bear to hold,
No room of my own, no place to go,
Except my rock, my quiet place,
To sit and watch the river flow

My peaceful willows speak to me
They whisper kind and loving words
They hold no grudge, they do not judge
Their branches sway with singing birds

The finches and the starlings chirp
The bobcats hunt along the path
The frogs are croaking in the mud
I cool my brow and calm my wrath

My peaceful willows speak to me
"Where are you going, where have you been?"
I am a wandering, homeless soul
My peaceful willows take me in

Poor Chuck.

We all work out the puzzle of life, day by day. Uncle Chuck's problem was, the last time his puzzle got tossed in the air, by the time it all came down, too many pieces were missing. His daughter, Jolene, was just trying to pick them up.

Chuck's body died but his story, his essence, his ghost, perhaps, followed Jolene Huffington (the new Jo Huff) and her mother, Nana, around, from Carmel Valley to London and back again. Always there, an insistent, humming presence. We do find out more about Chuck in this part of the story. He just plain won't cross over to the Other Side until he has had his say.

*"Anybody can observe the Sabbath, but making it holy surely
takes the rest of the week."*
— Alice Walker
In Search of Our Mothers' Gardens

January 11, 1964
Fox and Deke Come Home

Fox drove home from the cabin in Ben Lomond, trying like crazy to keep her eyes on the future and not, as it were, in the rearview mirror. Deke was here, *now* and, although not as anticipated, expected or wished for (a mere shadow of his former hot tamale self) he was here.

Be careful what you ask for. You just might get it.

At what cost? she thinks. I have regained my lover, but not, a husband, but not, married before the eyes of God and the State of California, but not really. Tate has her father and she is deliriously happy. I am in a sham.

For a couple of days of their time in the cabin, Fox half enjoyed Deke's company. She made an effort. They ate berries, made pancakes, had small, superficial conversations. She got used to his slow and gentle presence. It was stiff but friendly, like an arranged marriage, like they'd just been introduced. They weaved in and out of their shared space, not only in different beds, but different bedrooms, an unusual honey-moon. They discussed demographics. Fox tried to fill Deke in on the thirteen years of Tate's life. It was cool. It was civil. She even dropped that bomb about his taking over at Sweet Farm instead of "getting a job."

If he asked her about *her* life, she clammed up.

What's to tell? she thought. *I have done nothing but run Sweet Farm and try to raise this child. I have no life. My life was spent waiting for you to come home.*

Deep inside, her inner voices screamed, her psychic body vibrated, in color. That roller coaster shakiness, like she had when he first showed up at Sweet Farm in the fall, returned. As long as they stayed on the surface, she coped. When things got personal, nope.

Perhaps things will be better when he takes over my job. I can do something off-compound, like Nana did when things were so bleak with Charles. Her job at the Dream Catcher saved her sanity.

Deke, meanwhile, felt as though he were being relit, like someone threw a big pinewood log on banked coals. He was ecstatic. He kept a low profile, which was his way. Not on purpose. He was just that person these days.

He didn't mind not talking too much. He didn't like having to think up quick answers, being put on the spot. His thoughts ran along the right lines, with reasonable responses, it just took forever sometimes to get them to his lips.

What Fox didn't know was that *she* was not the only thought on Deke's mind. Oh no. Another face appears regularly. Deke had hoped his imaginary box filled with *his* secrets, stashed away in his imaginary closet, was strong enough to keep Daniel inside it and out of Deke's head.

But Daniel, the boy in King City with his, Deke's face and physique (the spitting image of the old Deke, it's true) kept climbing out of the imaginary box and visiting.

Not in person. Not that. Just a presence inside Deke's already jumbled brain.

It's the boy, Deke thought. It's one thing to have seen Madge, who awakened him to a lost period in his "quest for his brain," but the boy! That nagged at Deke's consciousness for a whole bunch of reasons.

First, he has a son. A son he can never see or tell anyone about. A 13-year-old son, named Daniel. Second, Daniel's conception took place while Deke was, basically, completely out of his mind, compromised by a brain injury and amnesia. He remembered nothing about the six weeks with Madge until he saw her last month and she set him straight.

Oh, he'd keep his promise to not make contact or try to see Daniel. He wouldn't want to come up against anyone named Big Bart, the man who thought he was the boy's father. But it stirred Deke up on a regular basis. Big Bart happened to be in prison, but that knowledge did not help Deke's imagination.

Out of the corner of Fox's eye, she saw Deke looking out the window at nothing and presumed he was brooding over her. She didn't stop to think Deke might have other things going on in his life besides the re-pursuit of her own red-headed self.

March 20 1964
The Vernal Equinox

An Excerpt from Stevie's Honors English Journal

From the Latin equi or equal and nox meaning night.

An Equinox is an astronomical event, when the sun crosses the plane of the earth's equator and makes night and day approximately equal in length all over the world.

At the equinoxes, the "edge" between night and day is perpendicular to the equator. As a result, the northern and southern hemispheres are equally lit.

The equinoxes are the only times when the sun is exactly overhead at a point on the equatorial line.

Equinoxes and solstices are related to the seasons. In the northern hemisphere, the Vernal Equinox (March) marks the beginning of spring and the Autumnal Equinox (September) marks the beginning of autumn. In the southern hemisphere, it is the opposite.

On the Vernal Equinox in days of old, Pagans celebrated the goddess Ostara or Eostre. Ostara's feast day, held on the full moon following the Vernal Equinox, was pretty much the same date as evolved for the Christian Easter/ Resurrection in the west. The Easter Bunny and Eggs are a carry-over from the pagan days and don't have much to

26

do with Christ ascending to Heaven, unless you consider Fertility, Rebirth and New Beginnings.

The Winter Solstice, too, has lent many rituals to Christian celebrations: the indoor Christmas Tree, decorations.

During the Roman Empire's conquests in Britain and Europe, from the second century B.C. to the fourth century A.D., they suppressed all kinds of seasonal rites practiced by the Celts and other religious groups with their own Saternalia, the ancient Roman celebration of Saturn, the god of plenty.

By the fourth century, Western Christian churches figured out how to incorporate their holiday with Saturnalia and other popular pagan midwinter traditions and settled on celebrating Christmas on December 25. (My research shows that the Bible doesn't give a date for the birth of Jesus and some folks figure he was actually born in the spring.)

Before the end of the fourth century, all the best traditions of Saturnalia—like giving gifts, singing, lighting candles, feasting and making merry—had become absorbed into the traditions of Christmas as it is celebrated today.

Encyclopaedia Brittanica, *Volume 23, Venal-Zither*

Equinoxes, solstices, Saturnalia, Christmas, Christmas Tree, Winter Solstice, Romans, Ostara/Eostre/Easter, Resurrection

March 1964
Fox Walks

Fox found myriad ways to stay out of Deke's path, but best was to simply wander off the Farm on a long walk. First, of course, she went down to the Schulte Road Bridge, to check out where her crazy late brother-in-law, Chuck, used to sit with his flask. She didn't know why she chose the bridge, but she got the point soon enough. It didn't matter where, she just needed to move. She was one pent-up woman.

At the Schulte Road Bridge, Fox scrambled down the bank to the left, where she and her sisters hunted for crayfish back in the day. *Do the girls ever hunt for crayfish? Why don't I know that?* Fox couldn't remember the last time she ate one. And the famous frog hunt scene from *Cannery Row. Where was that? Right nearby.*

She found Chuck's rock, the one in the poem he wrote, *My Peaceful Willows*, which the girls read at his funeral they called "the Gathering." The rock is hard to miss these days with CWH emblazoned in white paint.

Fox sat on Chuck's rock and remembered him: once her sister's true love, then, her burden, then, dead. She could see why he came here to drink. It's a perfect place for a snort. Privacy under the bridge, soughing breezes waving the willows around, critters crawling in the bushes, freedom from prying eyes and critical voices. She could just imagine him with his monogrammed flask, taking a swig, dribbling gin down his chin, having a smoke and weaving his way home in the dark.

The next time she headed out the door in walking shoes, she went past the Schulte Road Bridge to the end of the pavement by the campgrounds and then up the dirt road through the little neighborhood of Saddle Mountain to the march of Monterey pines across the top. At the pines, she remembered Deke telling her about one dream during his journey across the country to "find his brain"—something about her disappearing into those pines and coming up again under a baby blanket, humming, and becoming a baby, becoming Tate, but he didn't know that, and he kept trying to call to her but he couldn't make a sound, couldn't move because his legs were in molasses. It made her shudder. It made her sad.

She'd arise early to do her chores and walk for an hour before driving the Sweet Farm truck to Monterey Peninsula College, finally enrolled in classes for an AA degree in Art History. She had no idea what she would do with this half degree, but she didn't care. She went to MPC to begin her transition, whatever that was. To just get off the Farm once in a while. Change the scenery. Change everything.

And the MPC professor? This disturbed and confused her and filled up much of her walking time—punishing her reckless self.

Lunch with the professor was exciting: stories of his travels and entertaining descriptions of the great art exhibits he'd visited. She didn't have to talk about herself at all. Lunch on the school lawn with a gregarious man was such a novelty. And no drama, just his lazy southern voice and those penetrating eyes. A one way street. *No room for anything but himmety-him*, Fox thought. Which was fine. The less she had to explain about her own life, the better.

The novelty fizzled like a firecracker in the rain when he invited her to his apartment to see pictures of an art exhibit (that she might use for a paper she was writing, uh huh).

Her first clue about the ineffable wrongness of this? The one large room with an unmade bed in one corner and Pullman kitchen with dishes in the sink on the opposite wall. In the center of the room stood an all-purpose wooden table, piles of mail and loose photos and boxes of who knows what stacked all over with a tiny cave of space for one place setting at the other end, with, presumably, the morning's breakfast bowl and cup. A mangy cat slept in a basket of laundry by the door. Another cat sprawled in the unmade bed. It all smelled of stale milk and cat urine.

Fox, eyeing the room, contemplated the exit. Without pre-amble, the professor stripped her of her coat and threw her on the bed, which tossed a yowling cat and surprised the bahooties out of Fox. He removed his own coat in a flash and, in the vernacular of the day, jumped her bones. He tried to pin her down with one hand and get inside her shirt with the other. If he thought he was being romantic, he was off the track. She kneed him in the groin so hard his neck snapped back and he lost his grip. Fox slapped his amazed face and leapt off the bed in a fury. She couldn't flee fast enough. This was not friendship, but something else entirely, and she wanted none of it.

Dammit. Ew.

She dropped the professor's class.

Before Deke came back, all she ever thought about was Deke: his face, his movements, his blue jeans with the cuffs rolled up, his Red Wing boots. She remembered his arm around her in the night. She felt his unshaven, scratchy chin. She thought about their nights of passion and their days of constant and happy interaction, his secret kisses behind the barn. English Leather and the smell of bees in his hair lingered forever in her nose. It hurt down to her toes to think of riding on the back of his Blue Indian Chief, her arms wrapped around his waist.

When he showed up at the door like a specter last November, she was sort of ecstatic for a couple of hours. The day after, she scurried down her fox hole, still afraid to come out. Even after she agreed to marry him, she stayed close to the hole. Whenever she poked her red head out, when she laughed at a joke or smiled at Tate or her face lit up in any way at all, Deke mooned at her.

She slept next to the man who used to drive her absolutely nuts with joy, who, at one time in history, made her shiver and tingle just to look at his broody beautiful face; the man who made her laugh, listened to her complaints, reacted to her joys, knew her inside and out.

She lay there next to him. But it was not her Deke Harley. Not the man she loved, not anything like the man she loved—sparkling and gilt-edged. This man was soft and sweet, and it wasn't that she didn't like him. She just didn't love him. And she knew she wouldn't. She didn't *know* him.

In the bed, listening to his soft snurfling in the night or waking up to see his eyes gazing at her face or the way he watched her drink tea or read the Chronicle, it all had a certain hurt in it. It gave her a pain that made her body ache, like being trapped in a straight jacket. She felt "the claws," that feeling of restlessness, twitching, like you must escape your skin. Fox's nerves sparked and jumped and her hair flew flakes of copper into the air.

She wished she hadn't agreed to sleep in the same bed. Oh, he was nice and respectful, but she felt his gaze, the hungry bear, and she was never alone in the night.

What a joke, she thought on one of her walks. On all of her walks. *Thirteen years of lonely, and here I am, lonelier than ever, with the man who still loves me in my bed. I am a mess. I am an irony.*

Chapter Two

March

Virginia Smith, Reporter

Rita set the coffee urn back in its place on the Tea Room self-serve counter and wiped up the dribbles. She went to the front door, unlocked it and opened the top of the Dutch door, swung it out and around and hooked it to the wall. The sun twinkled rainbows on the dew outside and the air was crisp and clean. A sharp and clear March day.

The Sweet Tea Room smelled like cinnamon, sugar and chocolate and the aroma drifted outside as the fresh air drifted in. Other aromas mingled: Chicken Noodle Soup, fresh baked bread, orange marmalade bubbling on the stove. The morning sunbeam caught the swirling bakery mist in the air. Now, at 11, Rita was ready to open and share her creations with the neighborhood. The cinnamon rolls were particularly good looking this morning, with a nice crumb and a sticky, gooey, buttery topping.

A woman appeared at the Dutch door and said, "Hello." Rita said, "Hello. Come in," which she did. The woman looked a little nervous, so Rita offered coffee.

She looked familiar to Rita, but, a lot of faces appeared at the Sweet Tea Room door, looking for coffee, tea, donuts…

"I'm not here for coffee, but that would be nice. I'm here to see Deke Harley. I'm Virginia Smith from the *Acorn*."

"Oh! Yes. I remember you interviewed Fox a few years ago about lavender farming." said Rita, pouring coffee into a mug. *Heavens, what's this?* she thought to herself.

"True. Yes. I guess you're an interesting family. Now Deke."

"May I know why? I am his sister-in-law, Rita."

"Well, sure, I'd like to interview him for the *Acorn*. About his return. I've heard he's back after a long, uhm, hiatus."

Rita took this in and didn't like the word.

"And, why an interview? Who wants to know?" Rita, like all Wymans, protected Deke Harley from the rest of the world.

"Our community."

Rita, who is never rude, said, "I don't mean to be rude, but, why is Deke Harley's return any of the community's business?"

"You've got to admit, it's a story," defended the reporter. "It was a story when he disappeared, it's an even bigger one since his return. At one time, it was an open case on the sheriff's calendar. They looked for him for months. They never found him, now he's here. Yes, it's a story, alright."

Rita thought about this. "Do you have a card? I'll give it to Deke Harley. If he's interested, he'll call you. But, I doubt he'll agree to this. He's…I just doubt it."

Virginia Smith said, "Look, there's nothing but gossip out there now. Wouldn't you like to put that to rest?"

Sweet Tea Room
OPEN
11am–5pm
Wednesday–Saturday

Sweet Farm & the Wymans,
proprietors

Very Special Treats
for Tea Time,
Second Breakfast,
Elevenses
and
High Tea

Sweet Tea Room

Daily Menu

Two Soups   cup/bowl $1/$1.50

Mixed Green Tuna or Egg Salad $2

Sandwich of the Day $2

Muffin of the Day $1

Scone of the Day $1

Cake Slice of the Day $1

Pie Slice of the Day $1

Saturdays Only
Donuts, Cinnamon Rolls &
Croissants
50¢

Sweet Tea Take Home

11am–5pm

Mixed Treats by the Dozen $6
toads, popovers, muffins, scones

Saturdays
Cinnamon Rolls, Donuts or Croissants 50¢

Soup of the Day   1 Quart $2.50

Salmon Plate for Four $3.50
house cured salmon, biscuits or crackers,
clotted cream, thin sliced red onion, capers

High Tea for Four $3.50
2 scones, 2 muffins, 2 toads in the hole,
biscuits or crackers, salmon cure, lemon
curd, jam, clotted cream

Lemon Curd   1 pint $1.50
Biscuits or Crackers 1 pound $1.50
Jam   1 pint $1.50

Sweet Tea Time

11am–5pm

Tea or Coffee .... 20¢

Tea for Two $2
2 scones, 2 muffins,
clotted cream, butter, jam

Tea for Four $3.50
2 scones, 2 muffin, 2 popover
clotted cream, butter, jam

High Tea for Two $3
2 scones, 2 muffins, 2 toads in the hole,
salmon cure, lemon curd, jam, clotted
cream

High Tea for Four $4.50
more of the above

High Tea Cured Salmon Plate $2
house cured salmon, crackers, clotted
cream, thin sliced red onion, capers

March 1964
Monterey to Carmel
Stevie on the Bus

As usual, the young girl sat alone on the bus traveling home from school on Highway One south from Monterey to Carmel Valley. The blur of Monterey Pines and Cypress and White Oaks and Mercedes and Volkswagens and big Chevy trucks and sometimes a guy with his thumb out hitching a ride rolled by, unremarked. Her eyes looked straight through the scenery, as if it weren't even there. Instead, in the window she saw two looping scenes out of her little life so far. Sometimes, in her fertile mind, she acted out every roll—mimicked the voices, imagined the clothes, the lemonade, the boldness and then the shame.

Stefani Awena Michel, known as Stevie, and Steve, or even *Sam* (as it happens, her initials) for that brief moment in recent history, was almost over the reason for the adopted name *Sam* in the first place, although it clung to her shirt-tail like a needy cat. It whispered (meowed) in her ear—made her remember being a fool.

Here's what lingered in her mind:

Was she really that stupid, dropping incognito into a bar on Cannery Row and propositioning a Perfect Stranger? For, it was nothing short of a proposition. She knew it.

Let's re-phrase that—propositioning a Perfect Stranger who turned out to be her long-lost uncle, Deke Harley?

She had been on a quest—to enter womanhood with certain carnal knowledge, to keep it separate from love, if she could. At the time, Stevie pushed away all thoughts of risk and vulnerability, dubbed him *Adam* and herself *Sam* (anonymity was key) and presented herself to the man she had chosen to, in her friend Farley Simpson's eloquent phrase, acquaint her with the *joys of nookie.*

What *was* on her mind at the time was the discovery of him, this Perfect Stranger—and who knew how long he might be available? The timing was perfect (let's just say her monthly fertility cycle was not receptive—Stevie was up on natural contraception, at least in theory) and, she would be in Monterey job-hunting, allowing her to hide these bold actions, this secret encounter, from the Nosiest of Parkers (eleven at that count) living with her on the Sweet Farm compound—basically, her entire family.

Now, on the bus, Stevie faced facts: she was not *Sam*, Uncle Deke not her imagined Perfect Stranger, *Adam*; never was *Adam.* There is no *Adam.*

(New Year's Resolutions notwithstanding, she obsessed.)

And the two scenes playing over and over in her movie theatre of a mind? 1, Sitting at a table in a bar actually asking a Perfect Stranger to deflower her and 2, The moment she realized to whom it was she had made that request. [In case you've forgotten that, too, she threw up her PB&J].

Stevie was not only too young to be in the Outrigger Polynesian Piano Bar on Cannery Row in the first place (barely fifteen, looking somewhere between 10 and 30), but *nookie* with her could have put the so-called *Adam* in jail (sorry for the 60s teenaged vernacular again but, duh, that's why they call it jail bate). Stevie alias *Sam* would be in big trouble with her Aunt Fox and her cousin, Tate, not to mention her parents, Rita and Fáno, and…well, the law. The world.

She hadn't been "a woman" for ten minutes (the changes in her body were disturbing, exciting and dreadful) before she was out looking to get laid. She laughed only on the rare occasions when she wasn't brooding about her crazy behavior. She thought, *Maybe I am the one who needs a shrink.*

Fate was her savior, her deus ex machina, because she intervened and kept *Sam* (Stevie) and the imagined and fortunately reluctant and clueless *Adam* (Uncle Deke) out of each other's arms.

To Stevie, every bus ride home after school from Monterey was the same: an opportunity for her mind, full of muses and critics, to nag her. As Stevie said to her Uncle Deke when apologizing for her brash and forward behavior of last fall, "It's not the first time I let wild horses loose in my imagination, but it's the worst time."

Stevie thought her first novel could be based on the cast of conflicting voices in her head, knowing she was surely the only person in the land with this problem. When someone complimented or acknowledged her in some way, she wanted to say, "Oh, if you only knew what goes on inside my head, you wouldn't like me." And now this.

Getting over IT has not been that easy. Sometimes, Stevie imagined the muses (Patricia and Fly, her personal muse faeries) and the critics (myriad names, based on nuns and imaginary aunties too numerous to mention and all with pointy fingers and harsh voices) crowding around a big conference table, observing her through a one way mirror.

Good old Patricia, the queen of muse faeries, always there, cluttering up Stevie's shoulder. She fingered the strands of tiny pearls around her neck, clicking them, like prayer beads in the hands of the Buddha. She tapped together the heels of her little Mary Janes, like Dorothy and her ruby slippers. That's when a flash of creativity might blow in Stevie's ear like a tiny wind of bold ideas. It was up to Stevie how to use and manage these ideas. The muses remained neutral. Although, Patricia, prone to muse-ish laughter at Stevie's expense, cackled. Stevie heard it clearly, of course, Patricia hanging out so close to her ear.

It was not her intuition, or secret suggestions from Patricia or Fly that made Stevie walk into the Outrigger that day. Oh no. It was the stubborn goat. It was the girl who thought she was a woman, a woman who didn't need muses or guides or basic rules of behavior. She knew what she wanted.

Wow.

And the only person she could talk to was Farley. Good ol' Farley, friend for life. Thank God he wasn't even on the list of contenders for the privilege of exploring her womanhood. His friendship was gold, but it was best kept that way. Besides, a part of her felt so deeply humiliated about the *Adam*/Deke thing, she could sometimes barely look Farley in the eye. And he's the only other person in the world (besides Deke, of course) who knew of her moment of failure and embarrassment. Crikey, he could blackmail her.

In Stevie's mind, sashaying into the Outrigger to flaunt herself to a handsome older man for the purposes of unlocking the mysteries of her private parts topped her list of her life's regrettable moments.

"Crapola!" she said out loud. "Get over, over, over it!"

The bus driver looked up. Stevie looked down.

She re-read the first entry in the inaugural *Little Red Book*. The last line read, "There won't be much to write here. I'm only 15."

Right. She needed something to do besides brood.

March 1964

Stevie's Little Red Book

The Sock Hop

Ohh noo! What a mess!

I am lying on my bed, rumpled up with my pillows. Mesmer lies under the bed covers, her head on my ankle, warm cat breath on my bare skin, and every now and then, whiskers twitch and tickle. Misty, aged beagle dog, is on the floor, freight train snores exploding her loose jowls.

But, my mind is on other things. Tonight Farley screwed up our friendship, maybe forever. If I write it down, can I get it out of my head? If I express on paper the extraordinary grief I feel tonight, can I get up tomorrow and act like nothing happened?

Everything happened.

The worst thing happened.

The moment I've been avoiding for months snuck up on me.

Farley kissed me at the Salinas High Sock Hop! I never should have gone. I felt something going wrong the minute he picked me up in Phoebe, the orange truck.

He brought me flowers! All of a sudden, we were on a date. This was never supposed to happen. Just because two friends

44

go to a dance doesn't mean they are going steady, or even going out.

Farley is my friend. I want Farley to stay my friend, but now it's all complicated and upsetting, because of the kiss. If only he hadn't kissed me, I might have enjoyed the evening.

But he did. And, dammit, it was nice!

But, it can't be nice, or even halfway nice, because he is supposed to be my friend, not someone who is kissing me. Kissing is off limits, anyway! He knew that!

After all that Adam business, it turns out that Farley became my first kiss after all. Dammit, again. It definitely was not supposed to be Farley.

He looked at me all moony and love sick, and in an instant, everything changed. Paul Anka crooned Puppy Love *to Annette Funicello and we danced. We've danced before: jitterbug, the stroll or slow dancing in a lazy pattern, side to side, like all the kids. Farley's a good dancer, for a big boy. He does a mean Watusi.*

Farley's hand on my back felt different, full of sparks. His fingers tapped the Puppy Love *beat on my shoulder blade. Something passed from Farley to me. One minute we were laughing with Farley's football player friends by the gym bleachers, although why he hangs out with these guys, I'll never know, since he doesn't play or even like football and these particular football boys are rather unimpressive dufuses. The next minute we were on the dance floor with his hand pressing through my sweater into my backbone, his pretty brown eyes looking into mine (without his glasses, come to think of it, that should have been a clue). I will never get* Puppy Love *out of my head. Ever.*

His breath smelled all root beery and sweet, and his hand touched my face like a feather. It took a few seconds to realize what was happening. And I couldn't stop it.

I barked at him, "Crapola, Farley! Take me home!"

I heard my favorite new Beatles song, She Loves You, Yeah, Yeah, Yeah, *as I slipped on my Keds and made my way to the gym door and then to the truck with my eyes straight ahead and blinders on, like a horse, so I wouldn't have to look at anyone or see that they saw, or, knew, knew that I had just been kissed.*

Farley was all apologetic and sorry, but he was happy to be kissing me. He liked it.

I have lost my best friend.

So much for Resolution #3.

Tate just opened the sliding door to my room and came in because she heard Farley's truck in the farm driveway and she thought it was early to be home from the Sock Hop. When I told her the reason, she said, "You know, Stevie, for a smart girl, you do some dumb things."

I flashed her my indignant pout. She said, "Really. Farley loves you inside and out, you know that. You'll never find a better boy than Farley Simpson to hook up with. He'd climb Mt. Everest for you."

"We're friends, Tatie. It's crossing a line."

"Who says friends can't kiss? Or be together, in the end?
If you ask me, I'd like my non-existent boyfriend to be my
friend, too."

"Oh, you don't understand. Everything changes. All of a
sudden, there is this brand new thing between us, tense and
spiky. He's like, was like, an old shoe: he fit in a groove, like
a needle on a record. I don't know, Tate. Kissing just seems
to spoil everything. Suddenly, it's about IT."

"Hm. Did Farley say that? Does he want IT?"

"No. He just looked like a cat with a canary feather stuck in
his teeth."

March 1964
Sweet Farm, Carmel Valley
Tate and Deke Visit the Night

Midnight. Restless Tate lay in her narrow bed in her Barn Cube, 80 square feet full of the life of Tate Marie Wyman Harley, girl singer. Monterey Jazz Festival and Salinas Rodeo Posters covered the walls, rhinestone belts hung from hooks, three ring binders full of music filled the lower bookshelves. The rest held stacks of handwritten lyrics, geodes and feathers, the two Littlest Angel Dolls and their little trunks full of tiny clothes she and Stevie played with as young girls. A collection of heart shaped rocks were scattered here and there.

Tate jiggled one leg and then the other. She tossed this way and then that. The sheets tangled between her legs so she jiggled again. She turned on the little bedside lamp and picked up *Peyton Place.*

Peyton Place made her think about boys. She wondered if she'd run into problems with her band, the Boys.

Her mind wandered. *Who and where are those Boys, anyway?* she asked the moon, bright and grinning outside her window. *Where do I look to find the right mix? What instruments go with my guitar? My voice?*

48

Will it be boys? Maybe I should look for girls. Sometimes I think boys are stupid. We never let boys in the Hobbit House, for good reason. Boys always seem to screw things up.

Take Stevie and Farley. Everyone but Stevie saw it coming. Farley did everything but put a sign above his head: I WANT TO KISS STEVIE SO MUCH.

Poor Farley. He's been waiting for this since he was ten-years-old. If Aunt Nana were here, she would roll her eyes and say, "Love is blind and sex makes you stupid."

Judge Simpson, Farley's father, took a shine to Jock Wyman seven years earlier, when they were both guests at a "meeting" of the Pacific Biological Laboratory, a men's social club who "met" (read that: drank and partied) in the old rooms that once housed the real Doc Ricketts's Lab on Cannery Row. Jock, whose obsession with John Steinbeck was well known, fell instantly in love with anyone interested in, or living in the heart of, Steinbeck Country. The Simpsons were big in Salinas, and very much a part of Steinbeck Country.

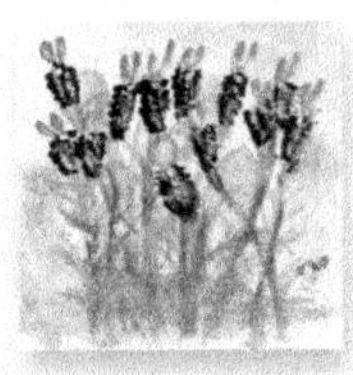

Tate remembered the day Farley's father first brought him to Sweet Farm. Judge Simpson came for a tour of "the scent" he said, in his gravelly voice. "It's not the same earthy farm smell as we've got in Salinas," he said. "Our fields have more manure in them, for lettuce and broccoli and strawberries. Our Simpson Warehouses, full o' strawberries red as rubies, smell so rich of earth and berry, it fizzes in your nose. Or the Fungi Farm, up the road. That wonderful musty, musky, moldy aroma. Here, it's all sweet and dreamy. It smells like a lady's boudoir." He strung that out. Boo-du-war.

The eight-year-old Stevie and nine-year-old Tate tagged along for the tour. Stevie stared at Judge Simpson's beaked nose. His tall lanky body, the judge-ish posture, managed to look all straight and regal, even with a tall man's stoop, like a great blue heron. She almost asked him how he knew what a lady's boo-du-war smelled like. It sounded personal. She'd have to figure out how to spell it so she could look it up.

Ten-year-old Farley was all arms and legs, gangly and pudgy at the same time, and nervous. The right stem of his glasses clung to the frame with a little brass safety pin where a tiny screw should be. He mooned at Stevie with those wide open four-eyes, like a be-spectacled and devoted cow. But she didn't notice. Our Stevie was focused since birth. Right at that moment, she zeroed in on the judge's nose.

The Simpsons stayed for tea, served by Rita on the little outside table overlooking the herb garden by the door to the Sweet Tea Room. Tate, Stevie and Farley, relegated to the picnic table out back, watched Fáno and Felix in the lavender fields and gazed at thermal-climbing hawks.

Gesturing toward the river, Farley said, "Have you ever caught mudbugs down there?"

"Mud bugs? Oh, you mean Crayfish!"

"No! Craw Dads!"

"Yes!" they all laughed.

"When was the last time you ate any?"

"Ew," one of them said.

They laughed and laughed.

Tate, Stevie and Farley chatted about the number of frogs in the Carmel River (too many to count, and slippery fast), and of course, the exact location of (and trying to imagine) the big frog catch with Mack and the boys in *Cannery Row* (the spot was right around the bend in the river, it always came up in conversation about the neighborhood). They pondered the names of the many Garcia children next door at Felipe's Produce Stand (Lupe, Gloria, Alfonso, Allegra, Carlotta, José, Miguel Ángel, Antonio, Francisco, Alejandro). Stevie mentioned burgers and fries. Farley asked, "Which would you rather be, a cowboy or an Indian?" All leaned toward the new term, Native American, although they didn't like the oppression of their spirit, and it was really their original ways that attracted them, so the question was changed to Indians before white men came in and messed with their lives and had to rename them Native Americans). For some reason, that led Stevie to the train to San Francisco (which they decided to do together some day); popsicles and root beer.

Stevie described to Farley and Tate her perfect day: lying in a hammock reading a novel, half in sunshine and half in shade, 70 degrees, lemonade with a long straw.

"What's the book?" Farley asked. At ten, he wasn't much of a casual reader but decided then and there he would read a stack of novels every night if it would impress Stefani Michel.

 She eyed him and said, "*War and Peace.*" Of course, she hadn't read it, yet, she was eight, she was still on *Nancy Drew Mysteries*, but she thought it sounded sophisticated. She saw him make a mental note, which went something like, *Oh Geez. War and Peace. That's like, a thousand pages.* But he didn't say it. *I'll never stay up with her, but I'll give it a go.*

From then on, those three were as thick as thieves. Stevie and Farley, though…there was something there from the get-go.

All this thinking woke up Tate completely. *I won't go back to sleep now,* she mumbled to herself. *Maybe I can go out on the deck without waking Fox and Deke.*

Now there was something to think about: Fox and Deke. In bed in the other room. Together. Like he never left. But better. They were married now and Tate was no longer a bastard. Now that she was no longer a bastard, she wondered what the big deal was. She didn't feel any different. She realized she really didn't care about the bastard part. But having her dad back, that was amazing.

Tate sat on the edge of the bed and put on red knitted slippers with black leather soles. She checked her clock—just after midnight. *Typical me,* she said to herself. She stood up, slid into her peacock-blue chenille robe, took the blue childhood blankie off the end of the bed and wrapped it around her neck like a shawl. She turned off her bedside lamp and tiptoed to the sliding glass door to the deck. She opened it slowly to keep it from screeching.

The lounge chair was empty. In the other chair, Deke's blond hair flew around his head like hay poking out of a loose bale, like that hot actor, Robert Redford, just out of bed in the morning. She imagined.

She quietly slid the door shut behind her.

"De?" she asked as she sat down in the lounge chair.

Deke, a grinning shadow in the dark, smiled at Tate like he'd just thought of her as a good idea.

"Tatie." He whispered. "I wondered if you were up. Then I saw your light come on."

"I'm up. I was thinking. And then, to stop thinking, I was reading *Peyton Place*. It kept me awake worse than thinking."

"I'll bet. I hear it's hot. Where'd you get it? Isn't it banned at Lucia?"

"Oh, yeah, well, it's circulating. One of the girls at school found it under her mother's bed. She's renting it out. Like, she has a waiting list and everything. A dollar for a week! She's a born promoter. She whispered around school about its being banned and all—it definitely is at Lucia School! She's got everybody all whipped up. Stevie gets it after me." She laughed.

At the sound of her laughter, a clear picture surfaced in Deke's mind of a man (the former him) and a laughing two-year-old (her) lying on the ground, watching the sky at midnight. He felt the pillow under his head, her little body tucked into the crook of his arm all wrapped up in the very blue blanket she had there around her shoulders. He remembered pointing out the stars and constellations. He remembered thinking, *She won't understand this. Maybe just the sound of my voice is what matters.* It made him sad to think the only thing she had to cling to for thirteen years was a two-year-old's memory of the sound of a voice.

"What were you thinking about?" he asked. This in itself astounded Tate. Her mother never asked Tate what she was thinking. Deke asked, and listened, and even whistled her tunes. He actually remembered.

"Boys. Well, not boys boys, but *the* Boys, for my band."

"Boys?"

The folks on the compound knew about Tate's goal for a band, basically two boys to play base and maybe harmonize with her. She turned pink whenever it came up. At sixteen, she hardly even knew any boys, except Farley. Santa Lucia School was gender isolated. And all that Junior Assembly/ Cotillion stuff made it worse, like department store mannequins, awkward wooden puppets. The dance monitors used 12 inch rulers to keep them apart. And she was always taller than the boys her age. And they never got to know each other. Pretty difficult, with a 12 inch wooden ruler poking you in the ribs.

But, they were too old for cotillion now and Tate was looking for musical boys.

"Boys," she said. "To make a band, Tate & the Boys."

"Ah. Tell me about Tate & the Boys."

He really wanted to know! Not to build a case against her

mother, but Fox just did not do that. Her questions usually focused on logistics: Where and with whom are you going? How and when are you getting home?

"Well," said Tate, "first of all, the boys have to be nice. I know so few boys, I don't know where nice ones are, but they need to be nice. And musical, of course. They don't have to be classically trained, but they should be able to read music. And, uhm, if it's going to be Tate & the Boys, then I have to be the lead."

Tate thought the Boys were late. She was almost 17, time to start getting ready to debut when she turned 21—at the Holiday Inn Lounge at the Beach in Monterey (she couldn't even go in there now for a burger without her parents). They'd better get practicing.

She knew what she wanted: two harmonizing, instrument playing, clean cut, handsome boys with perfect pitch to back her up without enormous boy egos getting in the way. She'd wear the sequins. The hat. Thank you.

To Deke, she said, "It's like this. All my life, I've been waiting. I've been waiting for you to come home. I've been waiting for Fox to notice me. I've been waiting to not be a bastard. I've been waiting for a chance to sing. I've been practicing (while waiting), because, I know it's what I'll do with my life. I've never wanted to do anything else but sing. I hate math, I'm sure I'll never balance my checkbook. I can't draw. I don't write. Well, I write lyrics. But that is the point. It's not just what I have, it's who I am. I've know this since I was five when I was still banging on the bottom of Mama Maria's soup pot with a wooden spoon. I need some boys to make me a band, and then I'll be ready. A couple of Ricky Nelsons ought to do it."

She laughed. This was the longest speech of her life.

Deke considered this as he looked at the sky, clear, deep and dark and crowded with stars. Tate was quiet, too, wishing the Boys would just magically appear so she could get on with it.

She looked up at the sky just in time to see a shooting star. They both gasped and laughed.

"OK, lead singer of Tate & the Boys. Looks like you might get your wish!"

First love is only a little foolishness and a lot of curiosity.
– George Bernard Shaw

March 15, 1964
Carmel to Salinas
The Kiss - Farley's Perspective

Farley drove back to Salinas in a happy haze after delivering Stevie home from the Sock Hop. He had finally done it. He kissed his Stevie.

And just as he thought, it was the sweetest moment in his life.

He had imagined the kiss all day. The tingle in his skin wouldn't go away, once he'd made up his mind. He would find the right time and just kiss her on the dance floor. He wouldn't ask permission, or give her any warning. That way, she couldn't fend him off.

Because, he knew she would. She had this high falutin' idea that they were in a platonic relationship and he wasn't supposed to think like a man, think of her as a woman. "Just friends," she said. "Best friends."

Farley thought if he just planted a sweet kiss on her beautiful lips, she might like it, and everything would change.

For the better. They could go steady, she could wear his ID bracelet or his school ring on a chain around her neck.

He never said anything. He just worked behind the scenes, maneuvering Stevie into his arms.

It has to happen, he thought, just before he called her the other day to say, "Steve, go to the Salinas High Sock Hop with me. It's my last high school dance."

And she said yes, because (in her eyes) they had danced before, it was no big deal. Farley would be in Berkeley soon, up to his armpits in pre-law courses and busy working for his father's friend, Judge Swann. So, of course, she'd go with him.

But he was 18, and she would be 16 in the Fall. No longer kids. No time to waste. He had to at least kiss her before he left for college. Then, maybe she would like it, and she would see him through new eyes. That's all he wanted—that she see him through the eyes of love. This had nothing to do with the *joys of nookie*.

Now, on the way home, he was bedazzled by the soft touch of her lips. It was more than he'd hoped for: warm, full of promise. It thrilled him down to his knees. It stirred his manhood and sent shock waves through his skin and made the hairs on his arms stand straight up. His soft dark curls sizzled at the ends, like he'd been struck by lightning. His horn-rimmed glasses fogged up from the pure emotion clinging to his eyelashes. He practically vibrated in the driver's seat, remembering the tingle, the sweetness, the rightness of it.

He knew she liked it. He could tell by the way she kissed

him back, just before she pushed him away and said, "Crapola, Farley!"

At first that made him laugh as he chased after her out the gymnasium door. He heard her favorite Beatles' song, *She Loves You, Yeah, Yeah, Yeah.* He sang it to her. When he saw, by the straight back and deliberate fast walk, that she was serious, she did want him to take her home, he was full of remorse and apologies, although he knew she responded like a woman should to a kiss. He could feel her lean toward him and lift her face. She denied it later, but he knew.

He drove Stevie home in complete, nerve wracking silence for the longest 35 minutes of his life. She hugged the door, looked out the window, emanating red hot steam through her very pores. The silence spoke.

When he stopped at the gate, just before she hopped out of the orange truck, she finally said, "Farley, this is a complete mess and I hope you feel awful about changing the course of our friendship forever."

"Stevie, I—"

She put up her hand in a flat palm gesture to stop any defenses or explanations coming out of his traitorous mouth. "Don't say a word. Words will only make things worse. I thought I could count on you. I can see that I can't. Don't call me later."

And then, of course, she slammed the door, which took some effort, her being 5 foot 2 and 100 pounds. The slam rattled the aged window and made the little dream catcher fall from the rearview mirror.

Farley admitted, to himself at least, that his apologies were shallow, since he was not sorry one little bit for that kiss. She was mad, but it wouldn't last. Stevie would come around.

She has to come around, he thought. *We've been best friends since she was eight and I was ten. There is no one else in the world I can talk to like Stevie. No on else I want. We are supposed to be together. I know it. And she knows it, too. She just thinks she needs an adventure. Or a Perfect Stranger! Geez.*

Or she's just being her stubborn goat self.

Dear Jo,

The unimaginable has happened. Farley jumped the line and kissed me on the dance floor at the Salinas High Sock Hop.

Please don't be like my other cousin and tell me I am stupid to not take up with Farley. I do not want to be that. With Farley. Doesn't every girl/ woman need a boy/man in her life that doesn't want anything from her besides friendship?

Now, I have to think of Farley not only as my first kiss, which was not in my personal plan, but as someone who wants to kiss me, period! I know, I know, just because he wants to kiss me today doesn't mean we'll be getting married and having babies tomorrow. It's not that. Let's just say, it's FARLEY! You know, Farley, whom we've know since we were 8 years old, like old buddies, like pals. It would never do.

And, everything brings me back to the Kiss: every idea for a story, every leaf I draw, every thought in my head, everything, and this ticks me off something fierce! I am so danged mad at Farley Simpson.

Love, Steve

April 1964
Honors English Journal

Peyton Place
Dying of Fame - A Book Review

Confidential for Sr. William

Grace Metalious has stirred up a literary storm. Peyton Place *is banned in many libraries and schools. The Dominicans have outlawed it from our school library as well as from our reading lists and declared it a sin to be caught dead reading it.*

I am reading it now. It is purloined (word of the week). Our schoolmate, BJ, discovered it under her mother's bed while looking for a missing bracelet. It was way far under, and dusty. BJ hopes her mother forgot it was there. BJ "borrowed" it. Just about everyone has paid her a dollar a week to read it.

I, at fifteen, have nothing with which to compare it. It is my first banned book. It is my first book with this kind of bad behavior by adults and their children, too. It makes Sweet Farm look like a host of singing angels live here in perfect harmonious bliss.

Grace Metalious exposes the minds of her characters, that's the most interesting and alarming part; all kinds of dark thoughts and scheming plans. She gets inside their heads and just digs in, sets up shop to probe their innermost beings. They all, all, are dark inside, from Betty Anderson, who uses sex like a power tool, to Selena Cross, who ultimately snaps and kills her raping and abusing stepfather.

Grace Metalious died in February, from cirrhosis of the liver from years of drinking. She was 39 years old. She said, "If I had to do it over again, it would be easier to be poor. Before I was successful, I was as happy as anyone gets."

I read an article that stated she "did not deal well with fame."

She died of fame.

Virginia Smith, Reporter

#2

On this rare occasion, Stevie was put in charge of Sweet Farm. You might think this a big responsibility for 15, and of course, it is, but the three girl cousins (Stevie, Jo and Tate) have been trained to be a part of this lavender world built by Wymans, so she is fine with it. And, it's Carmel Valley. And she'll most likely be alone for about half and hour.

Stevie chose the front patio of the Sweet Tea Room to take her stand, with a view of both Carmel Valley and Schulte Roads, the parking lot, the Tea Room, the Lavandula studio, and the Adobe House. If she looks around the back corner of the Barn, she can see her house, the Hobbit House in its tree and the Rodriguezes' cottage.

Stevie spread her school books out on the table, settled in. She had her tea, some new pencils, a fresh eraser and Volume 2 of the Enclycopaedia Brittanica, Antarctica-Balfe, for another lesson in astronomy.

She heard a noise in the Sweet Farm parking lot and looked up to see a red Ford Mustang. Too late to be invisible—she'd just have to deal with it.

It was an unusually warm Saturday in March, and Stevie was in the sun. She put her hand up to her brows and squinted toward the parking lot. A small woman, carrying a leather satchel over her shoulder and some papers in her hands, had just popped out of the little red car and kicked the door shut with her foot. Stevie did a quick scan.

Small person, 40-ish, bushy salt and peppery hair, black rimmed glasses, red lipstick. Calf-length skirt and brown boots, natty little tweed jacket. Nice.

Wait. I've seen this woman before. She's the reporter from the Acorn. Wonder what she wants, again?

Stevie put down her pencil and slid a piece of paper into the encyclopedia to mark her place. She stood up and went to meet Virginia Smith.

"Hi," she said, and put out her hand. Virginia rearranged her papers and satchel and grabbed Stevie's hand for just a moment, before returning her hands to the papers fluttering in the breeze.

"Here, set your things down," Stevie said. She knew Virginia had met with Deke a few weeks ago, but she also remembered something Aunt Fox said about the Sweet Farm interview with Virginia Smith a few years back. Fox said, "Virginia Smith doesn't give a fig about lavender farming. She was after *the story.*" They all knew *the story* to which she referred. Still the same story. New chapters, is all.

Virginia picked up a rock, put the papers on the other side of Stevie's table, placed the rock on top, set down her satchel and took Stevie's hand for real.

"Hi. I'm Virginia Smith."

"Yes. I know," said Stevie. "I'm Stevie Michel."

"Ah. Rita's daughter, right?"

"Uhm, yes, that's right."

"Sorry, I don't mean to pry. It's just that, I'm a reporter. It's my job."

"Ohhhkay," Stevie said, kind of smiling. "Then you *do* mean to pry."

"It's OK, it's OK, I'm not here to ask you questions. I'm just here to see Deke. Is he here?"

"Not at the moment. Can I help?"

"You can give him this, please. It's the first draft of the full article from our interview, for the *Acorn*, for his approval. Well, it's the second version of my article. I had to take out a few facts."

"Take out facts?" Stevie perked up. "Like what?"

"Aw, I guess it's OK to tell you. The more personal stuff. About Fox Wyman…and the daughter."

Stevie laughed. "*The daughter?* You mean, Tate? Why would you write about Tate? Or Fox, for that matter. This is about Deke, right?" Her braid quivered.

Virginia looked at Stevie. *Here is a tough little cookie,* she thought. *Not afraid to just say it.*

Virginia, also not afraid to just say it, launched into a defensive rant on the pros and cons of being a reporter in Carmel and what utter drivel the Living Section was and… she stopped blathering, thought about the recent conversation with her boss, wherein he said, "You can't print this, Ginny." She looked at Stevie, who scrutinized her while waiting for an answer. Virginia said, "You're right, Stevie. I have no business writing about Tate and Fox."

Stevie nodded. They talked about writing for a few minutes, after Stevie' hackles went down and Virginia let go of her Jack Russell Terrier demeanor.

The scene was more relaxed when Fox pulled into the driveway and recognized the woman immediately. She prepared to come into the scene like the protective mama bear she was. Stevie saw the signs: copper sparks, steaming pink face, frowning feathery red brows.

Dammit. What is Virginia Smith doing here? Bothering Stevie. Shouldn't leave teenagers alone on the Farm, Fox. She'd better not be worming information out of my niece.

"Miss Smith," she said. She sounded cold.

Of course I sound cold. I am a cold person. Just ask my daughter.

"It's fine, Aunt Fox. Everything is fine. Miss Smith was just bringing her finished article to Deke."

Carmel Acorn Article

Deke Harley did, after all, grant this interview to quell the gossip. Deke was tired of being *the story.*

We can just imagine Virginia Smith, Local News & Features Editor of the Carmel Acorn Weekly Review, breezing into her boss's office at 8th and Dolores in downtown Carmel and plopping her latest 1000 word essay on his desk (this would have been a few days before). Her eyes are wide open, her bushy, wiry hair all on fire. A gleeful stare penetrates the back of Templeton Jones's head, forcing him to turn away from his brand new IBM Selectric typewriter, face Virginia, sigh, smile, comb his fingers through his sparse hairs and pick up the stapled document. He read:

Deke Interrupted - 1st Draft

Michael "Deke" Harris Harley, sometimes known as Cowboy (if only for his fancy boots), has certainly seen some hard times, including his first twenty years of life in the Oklahoma Panhandle, dealing with mid-western farming gone bad.

His father Hiram's farming dreams were "doomed from the start," says Deke. Those speculators and "suitcase bankers" lured naive people like Hiram to Oklahoma with descriptions of bountiful farming in a Garden of Eden, then went back to their safe cities with cash in their pockets and had a good laugh.

"Sold them all a bill o' goods," Deke says. "Unworthy farming land in the first place, rendered downright useless by the greed and corruption of the Big A [Agro, he means:

agriculture on a giant scale], which stripped it of its feeble bounty." By 1930, the topsoil was gone with some mighty zephyrs and dust was literally the word on everyone's lips. The term Oklahoma Dust Bowl was coined by the press when Deke was a boy.

After a few years in the Army during WW 2, which he seemed to come through physically unscathed, the dispirited Deke found his way to Salinas on his 1940 blue Indian Chief motorcycle. While looking for a job, he drove to Sweet Farm out in Mid Carmel Valley, where Jock and Maria Wyman hired him to manage the business, cultivation and processing of their ten acres of lavender near the Carmel River. Deke got more than he bargained for, including the Wyman's youngest daughter, Fox, and a baby named Tate.

But here's where things get interesting. On July 10, 1950, Deke dropped his girlfriend, Fox (they were not married at the time) and their 2½ year old, Tate, at the Salinas Rodeo and drove off in the Sweet Farm truck to "run an errand." He never returned.

Well, he came back, thirteen years later, with a story.

The gist of it is, he woke up in a field with no truck, no wallet, no memory and a painful lump on the head. He wandered around the countryside for several months, trying to remember who he was and where he belonged, his only clue a half-written letter in his pocket to someone named Judge Harris in Maryland. The name meant nothing to Deke in his befuddled amnesiac state, but the letter suggested the judge might be a relative, so he worked his way to the Eastern Shore of the Chesapeake Bay.

During the telling of this long saga, Deke teared up several times. He took long pauses in his narrative to breathe, think and remember. His speech is deliberate, sometimes hesitant. He compensates, he says, for some permanent damage to the soft tissues inside his skull.

Deke learned to live by trust, since his lack of memory afforded him no past. He didn't know, but accepted, his mother, grandparents and great uncle, with whom he lived from 1951 to 1963, and did not know what he was missing in California, his Maryland family being unaware of his Carmel Valley connections, as was he at that time.

In 1960, he fell off a ladder and wound up in the hospital for the third time. He awoke from surgery recognizing his mother, et al. He also remembered a whole life left behind in Carmel Valley; interrupted, indeed.

Meanwhile, the Monterey County Sheriff set aside the case after a few years of fruitless searching. The Sweet Farm truck was dug up half under water in a ravine a few weeks after Deke's disappearance, the wallet found in Fox Wyman's room at the farm. Wherever he was, the sheriff said at the time, if he wasn't dead, Deke had made himself invisible. He had unconsciously slipped through the sheriff's hands, wandering off with no ID and, as Deke puts it, "half-a-brain."

Harley's now-wife, Fox Wyman Harley, says she didn't give up on him for ten years, because she "knew he wasn't dead."

This reporter did not ask how Mrs. Harley knew nor why she eventually gave up, but Fox Harley did say she was not really surprised when Deke showed up last November.

Deke Harley, a reluctant interviewee, declined to talk about his reception at Sweet Farm after a mysterious thirteen year absence. "We work it out one day at a time," he says. "It's enough for me just to be here with my Sweet Farm family."

He was, however, very happy to show me his 1940 blue Indian Chief, stored in a shed after his disappearance in 1950 and given back to him at Thanksgiving 1963 by the Sweet Farm family and crew, who had tucked it under a tarp for safe keeping. Deke says, "I guess it's all you need to know about whether or not they accepted me back."

This nutshell version of Mr. Harley's eventful life does not do it justice. Questions still abound: What did he do during those thirteen years? What is the day-to-day life of a amnesiac? What does his 16 year-old daughter, Tate (not available for this interview), think of her long lost father? Who struck Mr. Harley and left him for dead in a field in King City?

To protect the privacy of the family, we probed no further, but as an amateur sleuth, I want to know whodunit, don't you?

We most likely won't be satisfied, the statute of limitations has perhaps run out, and Deke Harley is not up to it. "It's been over thirteen years, Virginia," Deke said to me. "It's so much dust in the wind."

* * * *

Virginia vibrated in her chair. Templeton Jones's face transformed into a scowl while reading her piece. The tentative smile the boss had given her when she slipped in the door with her prize—the one and only interview granted by the mysterious and elusive Deke Harley—was gone.

"You can't print this, Ginny."

"Why not? It's such a scoop, Jonesie! It's the only one. I got this! It should be on the front page!"

"Well, *should* and *will* are not always compatible. I can't run this. It's too provocative. And they weren't married!"

"They are now. It's part of the scoop. Everyone wanted to know what happened to the guy thirteen years ago."

"Oh, you can run a story. But not like this. Tone it down. Don't mention the illegitimate kid. Don't mention the 'wife.' And don't poke around anymore. That case is closed."

"I'd say it's not. It re-opened the minute Deke Harley showed up at Sweet Farm last November."

"Gin, you've been here fifteen years, we are a small town newspaper—make it small news. Chatty stuff—who's getting married, who went to visit their relations in Saratoga. Rotary lunches, Kiwanis Pancake Breakfasts. Don't go all *Peyton Place* on me and start sticking your nose where it's not wanted. Write charming facts. If you want to write exciting stories, go back to Chicago. Or write a novel.

"And for God's sake, take that bit out about Big Agro, or whatever you call it. Geez, girl, don't you know your so-called Big A has big clout around here? You want to get us shut down?"

Virginia, a 45 year-old widow and mother of four twenty-something boys, mumbled creative invectives under her breath as she left the office with instructions. She knew a hot story when she had one. She disliked this approach to journalism. *Tone it down,* she repeated with an internal sneer. *Templeton Jones is just a chicken.*

But, he was right. We all know that. So by the time Deke read it, the article was indeed, toned down. And everyone was glad.

Life consists of what a man is thinking of all day.
– Ralph Waldo Emerson

It may be that the satisfaction I need
depends on my going away,
so that when I've gone and come back,
I'll find it at home.
– Rumi

March 1964
Sweet Farm, Carmel Valley
Deke Works it Out

Every day some nugget of memory broke its way through Deke's head, making him jump and exclaim, "Yreka!" (which he never got right) and scribble it down immediately. Good memories were hard to come by, and he didn't want to lose another one, ever. When he wrote them down, they were more likely to stay remembered.

The remembered things were often obscure and disconnected. He was thinking about his father, Hiram, one day when the recipe for lavender bath salts Deke concocted in 1949 came to mind. He clearly saw it on a 3x5 card, written on that old portable typewriter. He remembered the measurements and something about food coloring. He mentioned it to Fox, who said. "Oh, that!" and went right to the card box.

He couldn't put his finger on how that was connected to Hiram.

Deke's Lavender Bath Salts

8 oz Mason Jar

1 Cup Epsom Salts

1 t Baking Soda

3 drops Lavender Oil

Optional drops of Food Coloring for tint

And there was that flash of his life long ago with his parents and brother in No Man's Land, Oklahoma. He saw the red sizzling dust, the debris of sand blanketing his world, the roots of the wild grasses dangling through the cabin ceiling. He imagined the well wherein his father suffered a heart attack and died. Out of those details popped an image of himself walking along the railroad tracks east out of King City, when he didn't know who he was, where he was going or why he was going down those tracks on foot.

Deke's busy mind, pre-occupied as it was with worthy memories, tried valiantly to stay focused on the present.

If Virginia Smith were to ask the questions frustrating her as a journalist, Deke might have told her Fox was as nervous as a feral cat in a basket. That he was on his best behavior every dang day to win her love. He could tell Virginia he slept in the bed right next to Fox every night, but felt a land as big as Nova Scotia lay between them. She slept in flannel pajamas. She turned her back to him as soon as the lights were out.

He might say Fox smiled and laughed at his jokes, and encouraged him about becoming Manager of Sweet Farm, and acted as cool as a breeze about letting go of the reigns.

But, she did not re-engage with him. Rather, she was disengaging. She put in hours, planned strategies, made lavender oil, but her heart was not in it, in him or with him. Where her heart was, he hadn't a clue and he was certain he would be the last to know.

She obviously knew how *he* felt. She made sure they were seldom alone and kept a cool emotional distance between them.

And the boy. He had to let go of the boy. So much to think about, to remember, to keep under his hat. It's crazy, going from no life for thirteen years to this—so much action, every day, something…

Deke cleared his (Fox's) desk of papers and put up his shiny booted feet and crossed his legs. He leaned over and took his carved meerschaum pipe out of the designated drawer. On his first day in the office, Fox stuck a filing label printed with DEKE in lavender ink onto the drawer, her way of saying, "Keep it neat, Cowboy."

So far, the pipe, some aromatic tobacco and a box of Diamond Strike Anywheres rattled around in it.

At Stevie and Tate's request, Deke replaced his perpetual pack of Camels with a pipe on which he could chew when things got tough. He had to have something to do or he fidgeted. The pipe was a compromise.

As he puffed his beautiful pipe, he read Virginia Smith's story about his return from the presumed dead, and as he read, he was grateful, seeing that she did not write about his hard-won-but-nervous-as-a-wild-pony wife and innocent-but-in-the-middle-of-everything daughter. He did not want to make a spectacle out of any of this. He just wanted to be home.

For he knew now, Sweet Farm was home. Whether or not the woman loved him.

Stevie's Little Red Book
Peyton Place

Reading Peyton Place *has not helped me one little bit to get the idea of defloration out of my head. I was doing well, no internal histrionics for weeks, until I started reading.* Peyton Place *just stirs it all up again.*

Why. Because, although the author cleverly dances around explicit details, for a neophyte in the joys of nookie department, like me, it's enough to get my imagination going again. In both good and bad ways. It just preoccupies me. It's annoying.

When I am not pondering all the kissing and groping between the Peyton Placeans, of which there is a surplus, I am rooting for their success in life or screaming, "Watch out! Watch out! Don't trust that jerk!"

I keep trying to replace that memory, that Farley kiss, with something else. Who pops into the picture but Adam of the Habsburgs, my dream man! I have no one else to put in that dream, but Adam/Uncle Deke. Crapola.

78

He just appears out of nowhere.

Not that I want a boyfriend. After my experience with the imagined Adam I want nothing to do with boyfriends for a very long time. Boys. Men.

Don't even mention Farley. He should have known better.

Note: Reference New Years Resolutions #7 and #8

GET OVER IT

* * * *

The Carmel Acorn *article stirred up a little hornet's nest of activity around Deke Harley. Several people showed up at the Tea Room, hoping to get a gander at the Cowboy with half-a-brain. He knows all the best places to hide at Sweet Farm: the tiny bathroom in the barn, the fence at the cottage, the stand of willows toward the river, Chuck's Rock.*

He's hoping the "folderol" will quiet down soon and life can just get back to normal. The problem is, no one knows what normal is anymore.

Things can sure change in an instant.

* * * *

PS Sister William is reading Peyton Place *after me! HAHAHAHAHAHA…She'll have to read it by flashlight under the covers in her cell. BJ doesn't know where the extra dollar came from. Sr. William slipped her hand under the scapular of her habit, whipped out this little flat purse on a thin leather strap and pulled out a crisp new dollar. She looked up and down the hall before she pressed the dollar into my hand and slipped the book under her scapular, like we were dealing drugs in a dark alley. Sr. William walked up the hall with her hands folded just so over the bulge in her habit, like she was deep in prayer.*

I told BJ it was a donation to the cause of literacy and that I needed Peyton Place *an extra week.*

Chapter Three

April-May

On the Bus

Stevie sprawled in her favorite seat behind the bus driver and plopped her pack and books beside her. No one sat there if her paraphernalia filled the seat.

The topic for today (for the committee in her head): the secret she'll have to keep from her friend and cousin, Tate. Both cousins, really.

I can never tell Tate about Adam/Deke, therefore I can never truly tell her about why Farley was not meant to be kissing me. I can never say, "Oh, I want an older Perfect Stranger to teach me the way" without revealing the colossal mess I made while trying to do just that. Like, "Oh, by the way, the older Perfect Stranger that didn't work out? was your long lost father."

Stevie tried to look at it as simply her private business, but when they sat in the Hobbit House or on the Rock these days, with or without Jolene, there was a lot of teenaged pressure, not directly from Tate but, like from the collective, like, all teenagers must be doing this, talking about this, and so shall we: every little change in the body and every new curl and every cute boy and every dimpled cheek and who looked like the nicest and whom we should ask to the proms and the burning questions no one addressed.

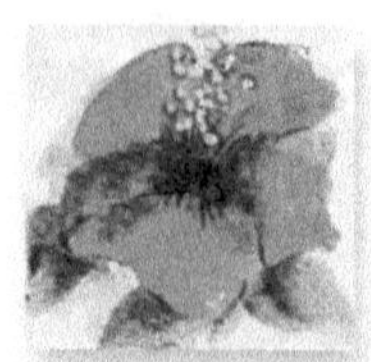# Meanwhile, in London
Jo Huff

Jo Huff posed in front of her bedroom mirror at Grand Mamá Charlotte's in full Mary Quant regalia: orange sleeveless mini dress, red and black checkered stockings and red patent leather chunky heeled boots. She tried to stuff her clashes-with-everything hibiscus hair into a cherry red beret. No matter what she did, the hibiscus tendrils spilled out in boingy kinks, like tiny Slinkies.

Upon seeing herself thusly decked out, Jo thought, *I look like a throw pillow.*

Well, Mary Quant herself says to dress to please yourself and to treat fashion like a game. So, here goes!

Trends were Jo Huff's life. Jo painted trends, ate trends, decorated her rooms (school, Grand Mama Charlotte's, Sweet Farm, her cubby in the Hobbit House) in trendy fabrics and designer elements created by the current fashion icons. Hey, she's an artist. Five days a week in white blouse, grey plaid skirt, navy blazer, saddle shoes and a beanie pinned to her hair? That'll do it.

She became her own canvas. Yes, the opposite of both her cousins, Tate and Stevie, whose idea of fashion was the comfortable fit of their jeans and "Do I have a clean T shirt?"

In 1963, Jo bought a leopard pill box hat, taupe Chanel style suit with requisite collar and lopsided bow, a string of cheap pearls and a pseudo ivory cigarette holder, in which she kept a candy cigarette. When not nervously chewing on the candy cigarette, she waved it around a la Audrey Hepburn. This emulation was short lived; Jo Huff could do little to hide her 38DDs and those boingy hibiscus kinks.

Stirrup pants with baggie sweaters and Capezio flats were the thing during her Christmas 1963 visit to Sweet Farm. And she still loved her embroidered black velvet jeans. But, Mary Quant called to her—those vibrant colors!

Jo was mad for trendy foods, too. Weekends "at home" at her Grand Mamá Charlotte's, Jo put an apron on over her latest homage to fashion, usually accompanied by red, white or black patent leather knee high go-go boots, and clomped her way into the kitchen to create elaborate trays of trendy appetizers or meals to eat in the TV room with her grandmother and her mum.

Jo posted recipe goals on the kitchen pin board. She intended to master British food, then move on to Indian.

Everything relating to food preparation was delivered to the back kitchen door at Grand Mamá Charlotte's, or purchased by the cook on her excursions around town. When Jo left on Monday mornings for school, a list for the following weekend appeared on the kitchen counter and if the cook was upset by any of this interference from Lady Charlotte's wild artistic granddaughter, she was smart enough not to let on. Let the crazy redhead do what she will on the weekend.

Jo Huff only admitted to her cousins her original reason for the whole cooking thing. Groceries were brought 'round on Saturdays from Morrison's by a young chap named Randolph De Smet, who timed his deliveries to the Huffingtons with Jo's usual Saturday morning home from school, because he liked her, while Jo timed her arrival in the kitchen by Randolph's deliveries, because she really liked him. She was up and (trendily) dressed and in the kitchen by 9.

She knew she looked fabulous, even if she did resemble something from Harrods bedding department. She liked the boldness of Mary Quant.

Her friend, Carla Pio, with Italianate dark hair and olive skin, painted her lips bright red, for courage. Her FACE, she called it. "Getting Ready" to Carla was "Putting on my FACE."

Jo chose Mary Quant clothes for strength. Her FENCE, she said. Jo liked Mary Quant, too, because Randolph De Smet once said she was so "mod." She wanted to be mod.

Here was Randolph ringing the bell. She caught her image in the small mirror on the desk and admired her sparkling blue eye shadow above her electric blue eyes. She sprinkled faerie dust in all that hibiscus hair. *If you can't hide it, flaunt it. Thank you, Mary Quant.* She grinned to check her teeth. Ready.

She flew open the kitchen door just as the bell rang. There was Randolph De Smet, 17 year old son of London tailor, Martin De Smet, known in the neighborhood as the *tailor to the elite.* Randolph, Rollie to his friends, wanted out of the neighborhood, even if it *was* filled with the elite. Well, *because* it was filled with the elite. Randolph was supposed to follow in his father's footsteps. Rollie had other plans.

Jo had an immediate plan. Rollie De Smet was drop-dead gorgeous, with the eyelashes of a girl and hair spilling over his collar in an untidy but graceful cascade of blond. Naive but organized and quite hormonal Jo invited Rollie and her groceries (raw chicken, eggs, oysters and whatnot) into her innocent lair. Rollie rested the market baggage on the kitchen counter, smiled at Jo Huff and handed her the bill and a pen.

"Thanks, then," she said, as she scribbled her name across the little paper. She returned the bill and pen to him, false eye-lashes batting like butterflies in heat.

"Nice outfit," he said.

Jo Huff looked down at her colors. Teasing or not? Just now, she felt a bit like the inside of an orange, and wouldn't blame him if he burst out laughing and offered to squeeze her into a glass.

Rollie smiled at Jo and said, "Really, it's quite smashing. Your colors are all…vibrating with the light."

She liked that, and said, "Would you like some tea? I came down earlier and heated the kettle."

"Why not?" said Rollie, and perched on a stool. He smelled cinnamon. This is getting interesting, thought Rollie, eyes wide at the bold clothing and abundant and twinkling hibiscus hair. And sparkling blue eyelids. He loved this girl already. They got along so splendidly.

Jo Huff Cooking Goals 1964

Cheese and pineapple on cocktail sticks
Angels and Devils on horseback
(bacon wrapped around oysters or prunes)
Cheese Straws
Pigs in a Blanket/Sausage Rolls
Scotch Eggs
Smoked Haddock
Coq au Vin
Chicken Curry
Duck l'orange
Roast Crown of Lamb
Macaroni Cheese
Nut Roast
Stuffed Aubergines
Cheesecake
Fruit Flan
Sherry Trifle
Pineapple Upside-Down Cake
Soufflés, hot or cold

Jo cut the cinnamon streusel coffee cake, still warm from the oven. She sat on a stool next to Rollie De Smet and crossed her red checkered legs just so. She did have a plan. That's one thing about our little troupe of cousins; they each, always, have a plan.

Rollie looked at Jolene Huffington, he knew she preferred this new nom de l'artiste, Jo Huff, and wondered at her choices.

They chatted for a while about color and then food and she shared with him her list of appetizers and entrees. They even talked a little bit about her crazy, dead father. She left out the humming apparition part, thinking it might scare off Mr. Gorgeous. But, she could stand it no longer. Her plan had consequences, and she was ready to get on. She wanted sweet, magazine cover romance. It so went with her outfit.

Jo Huff looked at Rollie and asked, "Will you go to the movies with me?" Just get right to it, Jo.

Rollie stared at her. He smiled. "Are you asking me out?"

She said, "Well, yes."

He lowered his voice, "Well, it's like this, honey. I'm a friend of Dorothy's."

"What?"

"Gay as a blue jay," he whispered. "But don't tell my dad."

"But," Rollie added, "I'll definitely hang out with you, honey. I liked you from hello. It's just…well, you know."

Jo knew. Plan foiled.

All she wanted was that Kodak moment. She had just the outfit. But, she'd have to get kissed by someone else.

April 1964
The Sweet Tea Room
Carmel Valley

Fox Considers Her Situation

Rita and Fox stood at the Sweet Tea Room counter discussing the upcoming birthday party for Jock, Maria and Stevie. The conversation devolved into running a cafe and its many morning chores: fill and heat the urns, turn on the heat, start the ovens, prepare the morning pastries (three made fresh daily!), slice the bread (made the night before), make two soups, defrost the par-baked scones and croissants, make sauces and chutneys and check the salad dressings, check the dry goods and the supplies…oh, my, the list was two miles long, the closing list even longer.

Fox was impressed, and glad Rita and Juana were in charge of the Sweet Tea Room. All she had to do was make the numbers add up at the end of the day. Fox really didn't think she herself would be very good at the service business. *Not only is there all this organization (and baking!), but it's such a people thing*, she thought. *I just don't like people that much.*

Juana slathered mayo on sandwiches with roasted chicken and pear chutney for Fox to share with Deke next door in the office. She wasn't looking forward to being with him in that tiny space, alone. She was building her own imaginary fence while trying to act all normal.

A small 40-ish Carmel Valley woman in a large straw Stetson-style hat came in the door from the table on the front patio and rather officiously, Fox thought, said to Rita, "My coffee has spilled."

While Fox checked out the local cowgirl, from new hat to fancy boots, Rita looked up, smiled in her most deferential way, picked up her clean white bar towel without a word and headed toward the front door. As they went out the door, Fox heard the woman say, "You might want to get it off my pant leg first."

Fox looked up from the woman's red rhinestoned boots to see how Rita reacted to this and saw her sister bend down and dab gently on the offending coffee-spotted pants with her towel and then get to the business of wiping up the spill, dripping off the table.

Like that, Fox thought. *I could never be that calm. Or nice. I'd hand the woman the towel and say, "Get it off your own pant leg, Penelope."*

And the latest hitch in the Sweet Farm giddy-up—this *Carmel Acorn Review* article. Right now, Fox liked people even less. And, even though Virginia Smith didn't invade her territory too much, she couldn't go to the grocery store without being stared at. She listened to the buzz—in the check out line the other day, when she picked up some last minute ingredients for Rita (items she had no idea what to do with: yeast, cardamom, shallots) she overheard someone whisper, "There's Fox Wyman. She finally married that guy Harley after sixteen years. Her child was a bastard. She shoulda married him years ago."

Don't they have anything better to do than gossip about me? I am not that interesting. Can we just lock the gate?

But nooooo, I am running a business (three if you separate Sweet Farm, the Lavandula studio and the Sweet Tea Room), learning to live with someone I don't love, rearing a teenaged musician who basically doesn't like me and planning a party for 100 people that will take over the Barn, Lavandula, the Tea Room, the whole compound.

Juana finished the sandwiches and wrapped them in parchment and handed them to Fox.

April 1964
Salinas to Berkeley California
Farley Leaves Early

Farley, upset over Stevie, who had not come around at all, signed up for early UC Berkeley classes and some hours with Judge Swann, his mentor for the next four years. This assigned by his father, Judge Simpson, and required, an internship—something like a serf.

How many times does he have to apologize to Stevie? Does he have to crawl on the floor and beg her forgiveness? He'd be happy to have it go back the way it was. At least he got to spend time with her, even if not in a romantic way. Now, she won't even talk on the phone at night, much less hang out.

He stopped by the farm to say, "Goodbye, see you in June."

She said, "You made a big mistake, Farley."

He said, "Please don't let it get in the way of our friendship."

She said, "It is very much in the way. It is like a roadblock, a knot in a hose, water in a gas tank, a moat with no bridge…"

He said, "OK, already. I get it."

Now, as he slid into the truck to begin his journey, he rolled his eyes. *Stevie Michel can be so danged much trouble!*

He left for college this morning. To Berkeley, early, he said, because he was ahead of his class and bored. To get away from me, I think. He could have taken the same pre-law classes at Gavilan in Gilroy until the Salinas High School graduation, but he was itching to split.

We haven't been hanging out. I just can't get over the kiss thing. Life is so confusing. I wanted one guy to talk to not interested in the boy/girl thing. I took it for granted with Farley. Boy (ha ha), was I wrong.

We are hardly speaking. He'd like to be speaking and, I surmise, doing a lot else because, since that Jack-in-the-Box opened, with the kiss, it's like I've been trying to shut it and he keeps letting loose the lid and out pops all this messy lovey stuff. He said it wasn't about sex at all, but because he loves me. That's almost worse.

He says he'd be happy to be friends again, and that he's sorry, but, really, I don't see the way of it. You can't retract a kiss. It's like stuffing a Jack-in-the-Box back in. It's always there, waiting to pop out.

Thank God I never kissed Adam/Deke. I could never stuff that back in the box.

Fox Plans a Party

Fox convinced Rita not to cook for the Party. Her final point: Rita might actually enjoy the role of guest, rather than managing food for 100+ people.

How little Fox knew her sister; the role as cook was the protective barrier—something to do, somewhere to be, rather than getting stuck in a circle of big people looking down at the 4'10" Rita. It hurt her neck, made her want to run down Fox's imaginary hole. Parties were the perfect opportunity for inebriated big people to pat Rita on her head of fluffy platinum curls. It made her feel like a puppy.

But Fox didn't think about any of this as she planned the event to honor the three birthdays. Fox's mind was on the big picture. She leaned over the counter in the Tea Room with a bird's eye view of Sweet Farm drawn on a piece of butcher paper spread out in front of her, the food and beverage stations mapped out. The list of party rentals on her clipboard grew by six more tables and twenty more chairs. She thought, *If this bash gets any bigger, I'll have to rent a hall. If it rains, I will cry.*

I should do a little historical display for each of them: Poppy, Mama, Stevie.

Party A List
as of April

Jock	Charlotte
Maria	Rebecca
Rita	Juana
Fáno	Chico
Stevie	Felix
Farley	
Judge Simpson	
Annie Simpson	
Karen Simpson	
Johnnie	
Fox	
Deke	
Tate	
Sadie	
Nana	
Ace	
Betsy	
The Smiths	
Will	
Jo	

May 1964
The Santa Lucia Senior Prom

 Tate

The Prom site was a masterpiece, themed "Alice," and a Wonderland it was, with lit magnolia trees and, high along the gymnasium ceiling, blue silver crepe paper balls bobbed on wires. The bleachers, pushed back as far as they would go, dripped with gauzy fabrics and garlands of white and silver and blue flowers and glimmered with strings of big white lights.

Each table of four or six or eight dripped with gauze and gleamed with rented pseudo silver and crystal. In the center of each table rose thin, silver-sprayed Madrone branches with tiny twinkling crystals glued on the branches and ends.

Tate looked around at the Santa Lucia girls in all their Wonderland dresses and their dates in awkward fitting tuxedos and was proud of their Promscape. The senior class was small, only sixty, and more than half showed up, except the postulants, the junior nuns. About thirty out of 55 of Tate's Junior class hosted the Alice In Wonderland Prom, which Tate Wyman Harley (co-chairperson of the event) thought up one night lying on Stevie's bed in her Alice Pajamas.

The giant cut-out of the Mad Hatter loomed over all with

a maniacal look on his face, a cardboard Alice perched on a basketball hoop, and at the other end of the gym, the cut-out Queen of Hearts pointed at the dance floor shouting, "Off with their heads!" Her huge mouth was open and the words spilled out in a big bubble.

Tate had gathered every ounce of courage she could muster, which wasn't much when it came to boys, any boys, musical or otherwise, and asked the brother of one of her school friends to the dance. His name was Todd, she hardly knew him, but he was safe and everyone thought it so perfect: Tate and Todd. For the weeks before the dance, the girls at school sang, "Tate & Todd, sitting in a tree, K-I-S-S-I-N-G!" over and over, ad nauseam. By the time of the dance, Tate wanted to cancel the date and skip the dance, so tired of the jingle was she. She didn't admit to any of those girls that she'd never had a date before. Much less kissed a boy.

But Todd showed up to meet her at the dance in a tux and he looked really nice next to her, in her pink voile puffy-sleeved "Alice" dress, for the picture. He quacked like a duck when they posed with the White Rabbit, who turned out to be the 70 year old and very proper Mrs. Shedlosky, in a fluffy bunny suit. He put his arm around her and squeezed her waist, thinking she was one of the students. Mrs. Shedlosky was not amused, and glared at him through her rabbity eyes.

Sadie, dressed in pale blue and her own version of puffy-sleeved Alice, was Tate's real date for the night, since they were both scared to death of boys and stuck together like paste to paper. She noticed Todd and her own date, Rodney (*Oh no, Todd and Rodney. Todney and Rodd. This is bad already*) had arrived together. Tate and Sadie came in the Sweet Farm truck, planning to take it back to Sadie's for a sleepover after the prom. The girls had their safety net all worked out. Escape was handy, Tate had the truck, and they were together. All was well.

And at first, all *was* well with the boys. The four of them ate their dinner by the light of the flickering decorations: breast of chicken with cream sauce over rice. Sparkling apple juice in goblets. Chocolate Mousse. Conversation was stilted. The girls were nervous, the boys were cocky to cover up their fear of these two popular but mysterious Alices, one pink, one blue.

The boys barely attempted to dance and soon gave up. Tate and Sadie gave *them* up and jitterbugged together. They sat out the slow dances, having issues with their errant dates and wishing they were home. Things careened downhill.

"Why don't they dance?" Sadie said between shimmies. "Aren't we good enough for them?"

"I don't know. Maybe they don't like it." Tate giggled. "Maybe they don't know how?"

"Well, why come to a dance if you don't want to dance? I could have worn a tux and saved us the trouble."

Tate looked over at the two boys, coming back in the door. What were they doing out there?

As the night wore on, both Todd and Rodney got ripping drunk from the shared flask of 150 proof rum (tucked neatly into the pocket of Todd's rented tuxedo) and high on Heaven knew what else. Every time the girls danced, Todd and Rodney slipped outside for a snort or a toke or a sip. They hardly said "Boo" to the girls on these ins and outs.

On one such moment upon leaving the table, the tablecloth caught in the hook on Todd's cummerbund. He didn't notice. When he stood up, he took the tablecloth and all its accoutrements with him. By then the dishes had been removed and for the fake champagne they were using plastic goblets, but there were sparkles and broken branches and cutlery everywhere, impeding diners and dancers alike. Still, he didn't notice. Todd and Rodney slid out the door like hysterical thieves, the tablecloth dropping to the floor in their wake.

By the time Tate and Sadie righted everything, which took a while since there were many little parts to sweep up, Tate was completely finished and suggested to Sadie, "Let's tell these idiot boys goodnight," for which Sadie was only too ready.

"Are you sure you want to leave, Tatie? You planned this whole thing!"

Tate said, "Oh, the fun was in the making. This part isn't the least bit fun. Let's go."

The boys barely noticed that. To their amazement, suddenly Tate and Sadie vanished.

The girls drove home to Sadie's and stripped off their poofy petticoats, donned pajamas and slipped into Sadie's double bed, talking all the while about the beautiful creation of the Alice Dance and the half ruin of it by the boys' bad and disappointing behavior. Sadie's parents, not expecting them home from the prom until midnight, were out. Tate got up and called Fox from the kitchen wall phone to check in.

"How was the dance?" asked her mother.

"Boring," said the daughter.

"That's too bad. What happened to your dates? Why are you home early?" probed the mom.

"The dates couldn't or wouldn't dance and we came home. That's all." They soon stopped the call in their usual stiff manner. Tate got back into the bed.

All was quiet. Sadie, partied- danced- and talked-out, snuffled on her pillow next to Tate, the night owl, who read *Life Magazine* with the bedside lamp on low. She was totally absorbed in Barbra Streisand's evaluation of herself. In high school she'd had no dates and no friends. She'd lock herself in the bathroom, smoke, glue on false eyelashes, emote TV commercials in the mirror, and dream of becoming a Great, Great Star. She said, "I hadda be great. I couldn't be medium. My mouth was too big." *Wow*, thought Tate. *She knew she'd be a Big Star. She knew it.*

A tap on the window popped Tate out of her Big Star reverie. She punched Sadie in the arm and woke her up. "What?" Sadie asked, "What?"

"There's someone outside," Tate whispered, shaking. Sadie heard it, too. Then they heard Todd's voice, whispering through the partly open window.

"Sadie. Tate. We came to apologize. Open the window."

Tate's heart stopped pounding against her chest wall. Sadie sat up and pulled the covers to her chin.

Tate put on her robe and tied the belt before she went to

the window and bent down to the opening. "What are you doing here?"

"We came to apologize. Open the window, please?"

Tate looked at Sadie, who shrugged. It's not like they didn't know these boys. Their families knew each other. They weren't dangerous. Tate slid up the window sash and opened the screen. The boys climbed right in, which shocked Tate, but for some reason, she started giggling. Adrenaline still whacked around in her system.

Todd held an open bottle of champagne with four waxed paper cups wobbling upside down on the neck. "We came with a peach offering." He actually hiccupped. "Peace."

Hm, thought Tate, *not sober yet.*

Todd poured four cups, with Rodney weaving behind him, a drunken, grinning hyena. Tate frowned.

Todd offered the girls each a paper cup. "They're Mimosas. T'you, and yer prom!"

Sadie noticed the boys weren't drinking, but took several sips, didn't like it and set down her cup. She eyed the boys.

Tate took a sip, then another. It tasted like Tang. Because she was thirsty, she gulped more and immediately got woozy. Then the room spun in little swirls. The empty cup dropped to the floor. Sadie held out her hand and Tate took it, wobbling to the bed to lie down. Sadie sat with her, in a dream state. Tate saw stars and moons fading in and out and the pink flowered wallpaper wiggled like the mirrors at the fun house.

The boys. Were these The Boys? No! Look at them! These boys were giggling now, unattractive drunk/stoned/high/stupid giggling boys.

They were not apologizing! They wanted to stick it to that stuck-up Tate Wyman, who ditched them at the prom. They just wanted to *freak her out.* Sadie, too, but Tate especially. She called them "idiots." Todd heard her.

They egged each other on and filled themselves with more and more bravado, but not champagne and Tang. Never that. That was for the girls.

Sadie was scared. Tate was in and out, unfocused. Her eyes fluttered and rolled back in her head. She looked at Sadie and blinked. What was in the champagne?

Just like that, the boys were on them, like crazed bees to surprised flowers, slathering wet kisses on their faces and groping inside the girls layers of robes and pajamas while fiddling with their own rented dress-up clothes. For a few more minutes, Tate was oblivious. Sadie, more aware than Tate with much less of the laced champagne in her system, wriggled her way out of the drunken heap of boys on girls, and ran to the phone in the kitchen. The boys took no notice, focused as they were on Tate. Things were out of control.

They just wanted to scare her.

Sadie didn't know where her parents were, so she called Stevie, proofing a term paper at the kitchen counter in the Chapel House.

"What? No! Oh God. I'll get Deke and Fáno. We're coming."

May 1964
Carmel Valley Village
Deke, Fáno and Felix, Heroes

Usually the one in slow motion, Deke Harley lost no time. His voice, his demeanor, his very presence lifted a notch, his nervous system kicked into high gear. *My daughter. My daughter.*

"Felix, you drive. No, Stevie, stay here by the phone, and tell your grandmother what happened. Get Fox up, now. Jock, give Felix the keys to the Cadillac."

And they were gone.

It took seven agonizing minutes to get to Esquiline Drive in the Village. Felix had never driven the big-finned boat of a Cadillac before so, in addition to being jacked up with potential rage, he was nervous about sitting behind the wheel of this vehicle, Jock's precious finned Cadillac. His driving was slower than usual, Carmel Valley Road was curvy, and it didn't help to have Deke Harley, furious that he couldn't drive, pounding his knee with frustration, murmuring, "Hurry. Hurry." Fáno reached over from the back seat to keep his hand on Deke's shoulder.

Deke's mind raced, his heart pounded like a hammer, his brow dripped with raging sweat. His thoughts ran amok, a merry-go-round of crazy pictures: his daughter, his Tate, and Sadie, too, mauled by two boys, their own dates for the prom! How could this be?

He forced himself to stay in the present, to be strong, to

focus. *What next? What do we do now? Get there, just get there and you'll know what to do.*

They arrived at the Campanella's house to see Sadie huddled by the front door, waiting, backlit by the living room chandelier, ethereal, vibrating and orphaned—the thin blanket over her shoulders, bare feet, dark hair flying.

The men whooshed out of the car and moved up the steps. Deke touched her on the arm and Sadie barely had time to say, "They locked me out! They locked the window! Down that hall to the right."

After they kicked open Sadie's bedroom door (one, two, three!), they pulled the two boys away from the groggy Tate, who cried and yelled and kicked, using her guitarist's fingernails to scratch. She was still in her pajamas. The boys were half out of their rented tuxedos, getting ready.

They tried to escape, but drunkenly tripped over their half-off pants, and by then, Fáno blocked the window and Felix barred the door, while Deke assessed the two idiots.

Sadie slipped beside Felix through the bashed-open doorway and pulled Tate out of the room. Together the two girls ran to the living room and cuddled up on the couch, shaking. Tate was still in La La Land, seeing double, feeling woozy, breathing hard and sweating *like a damn boy*! she thought.

Deke grabbed first one kid by the collar and then the other. They weren't such big boys to begin with, and now they shrank in fear. He had one in each of his big hands and bashed their heads together. He held them easily, scared the bejesus out of them with the fierce power of a lion, threw them on the bed, said with a roar even he didn't recognize, "Give me your phone numbers," which they did lickety split, for they were only seventeen, stupid, drunk and high and didn't want to die by Deke's bare hands there on the bed in Sadie's pink room.

Deke instructed Felix and Fáno to guard the boys, which they did with great pleasure, continuing to build the general power-of-wild-animal phantasm. Deke went to the living room, checked on Tate and Sadie and called the boys' parents, looking at his palm where he'd tattooed the numbers with a ball point pen.

He considered tying the little shites to chairs, maybe without their rented pants, until their abashed parents came, but he saw that Felix and Fáno had it under control. The boys sat on the edge of the pink bed, weaving, trembling, crying, mumbling, "We didn't mean it. We didn't mean it!" Fáno sat on the windowsill with their shiny rented shoes and Felix leaned against the wall by the door, so Deke spent the time with his arm around his daughter.

He was as calm as could be. The boys were practically wetting their hired pants.

Fáno said, "It's like having the old Deke back."

Felix said, "Better."

✳ ✳ ✳ ✳

Later, when Tate's voice returned and the shaking stopped and her vision improved and she was home in her own bed with a cup of mint and lemon balm tea with a parent on either side and Stevie at the foot of the bed holding her feet, she said, "De?"

"Yeah, darlin'?"

"How did you do that?"

"What do you mean?"

"Well, your…you…hmm. You were like Superman. You got bigger and fiercer and I didn't think you…well, you're not exactly…"

"Hghmph. Fit? Young anymore? I'm slow? I know I'm a softie these days, hon, but I'm a dad. No one messes with my daughter." And he flashed her that smile.

It was true. He had loomed pretty large back there. It took a lot out of the man, which he didn't admit to anyone on the compound. It was worth it, although he spent the next two days napping.

Jock, in bed with Maria in the Adobe House, said, "I can't help but wonder how we would have dealt with that without Deke."

The similar predicaments, hers with the professor, Tate's with the boys, was not lost on Fox for one moment. *If it weren't my own secret,* Fox thought, *I would tell Tate about the professor and show her how I kneed him in the groin with great accuracy.*

Oh my God.

Tate escaped rape. This is not funny. And, dang, Deke came to her rescue "like Superman," she said.

"You should have seen him, Stevie," she said. "He was amazing. He took on those boys like they were little rag dolls. He was as calm as could be, but kind of grew big, like the Hulk. Todd and Rodney were scared to death. They deserved it. I hate them for this. They kept saying they didn't mean us harm! Can you believe it?"

"I know," I said. "Chloral hydrate! Where did they get it?"

"I don't know, but I'll bet they won't do that again. They'll have a hard time showing their faces at their schools, 'cause Deke says he'll tell all the parents everywhere he goes. Marilee must be mortified to have Todd as a brother."

She made it sound funny, but she is shaky and has bad dreams and is afraid to be alone.

About these two boys, Todd and Rodney. How does it happen that two boys you know can show up and "slip you a Mickey?" Who does that? Didn't they think they'd get caught? Were they thinking with their wienies? Or were they really that vindictive? Or that drunk and stoned? Or just plain stupid?

Tate said the four parents showed up and they had a little Pow Wow there in the middle of the Campanellas' living room while Felix and Fáno stood over the boys like "big ol' German Shepherds" in the other room. When the Campanellas came home giddy from a date night, they sobered up in a hurry. What a scene. I wish I'd been there. No, I don't.

The boys were too smashed to even apologize, because by then the powerful cocktail they were on turned to toxic poisons in their heads and, as Tate said, "made them even stupider."

They kept repeating to Fáno over and over, "We weren't gonna do it. We weren't gonna really do it." Sounds to me like they were pretty close to "doing it."

I guess the parents felt like complete failures in the parenting department by the time Deke got through with them, and he sent the boys home only because they are seventeen and stupid and drunk. He said he won't report this (although we know he's already planning to tell Sheriff Lovell, his buddy) as long as the parents punish them in some meaningful way and that they come to Sweet Farm with their parents, in person, sober and in the light of day, to apologize to Tate and Sadie.

Dang! That Deke.

He looked really wiped out by the time they got home.

I am worried about Tate, too, trying to act all normal, like nothing just happened to her. I can't imagine she is unaffected by this. I think she's holding it in. Pretending.

I can't say what I would be like, drugged into a stupor, but I know I would be blazing mad, after. Not just about the drug, but about some jerky boy taking my virginity. Or even almost taking it in this case, but only because they were too drunk to unzip their twenty dollar pants.

They "didn't mean to do it."

Right.

Definitely not in the "Beautiful first time" department.

Part Two

Chapter Four

June

Stevie asks Maria

Maria Wyman was seldom speechless. Oh, she knew when to keep her mouth shut. When necessary, she picked up her knitting and buttoned her lip. Maria had a great sense of dignity. And a very private past.

So, when Stevie asked her grandmother the question, the pause in conversation was palpable, the sound of silence a trombone in her ear.

"Pardon, cherie?" she said, to garner some time.

"Sex, MM. No one else will talk to me. I thought you might tell me what it's like. Especially the first time. I need to know. I have my reasons. And I have a dearth of information."

"I see," said the French grandmother, biting her lip. Maria's quick responses crashed around in her mind.

The two were sitting in the matriarch's bed, cuddled up with hot chocolate and *War and Peace,* believe it or not—Stevie thought she'd better read it and quit pretending she had. It was Stevie's turn to read aloud. She read the page describing the young daughter of a Count who was "just at that charming age where a girl is no longer a child but that child is not yet a woman."

Stevie stopped reading, put her bookmark in place, closed the book, set it on the bed and looked at her grandmother.

When she asked the question, she had tears in her eyes. Her grandmother took this question seriously. Quick responses were useless here.

"Did you fall in love with Poppy first, before you had sex? Was he your first time? Did you like it? How old were you? I know I'm young, but, after That Night for Tate, and…and… some other things, I want to know more about it. Like, who do you trust? And if it's natural and easy or awful or disgusting or is it about love, which I personally don't think it is. You know. I have been trying to work it out. I…I just want to be informed, is all. I lead a sheltered life. And I want a Beautiful First Time."

Mama Maria rolled up her grandmother sleeves and prepared to tell her own story. It was time. It was a long story, but they had all evening. And it was all she could contribute to the subject, the very personal subject, of "the first time."

Flashback 1912
Wherein we finally
learn something about Maria

Young Maria Pelletier, with her art teacher, Madame Rocha, and three other budding art students, rode the train for two and a half hours from their little village in the Loire Valley to Paris. Their goal, to view Marcel Duchamp's controversial oil painting, *Nude Descending a Staircase*. The cubists said it was even too cube-ish and futuristic for them, and rejected it. Madame Rocha was curious, and gave the girls an opportunity to accompany her to Paris.

They toured other galleries and exhibits and critiqued *Nude Descending a Staircase*. Our Mademoiselle Maria Pelletier thought it looked like a complicated musical instrument.

The troop of young country artists stayed in a grand hotel, ate oysters and caviar and sipped champagne from thin crystal flutes at a small gallery owned by a friend of La Rocha.

The Rock, fierce protector and shepherd, herded the little flock of artistic virgins from the country, whose eyes she would open and whose pantaloons she wished to keep together.

While in Paris, someone of significance noticed the seventeen year-old Maria Pelletier, gliding down Boulevard Saint-Michel behind a gaggle of chattering girls and Madame Rocha in attendance.

Couturiere Lucy Duff-Gordon, whose designs wowed the world under the name of *Lucile*, observed Maria from her perch on the balcony of the Royal Saint-Michel, where she ensconced her grand self while preparing for a trip to the United States aboard the unsinkable Titanic. Before she left Paris, she wanted three new mannequins to train for the New York Salon. She had invented the whole "mannequin parade" thing and needed new faces, new girls. She searched for months and she was tired. When she looked up and observed the tall, elegant girl with the profile of a Greek goddess and long black hair pulled back in a loose pony, she gasped, "There is number three. Gaston!" she cried to her companion, "Go get me that girl." A long manicured nail at the end of an elegant finger pointed down to the street.

A breathless Gaston returned twenty minutes later, his purple corduroy suit ruined with sweat! He ran like the wind to catch up with those girls, but failed to persuade Madam Rocha that he was not out to molest our Maria. He was as flighty as a butterfly, in his purple beret and matching scarf and jacket and pants, but his curling moustaches exuded a threat nonetheless, at least to the over-protective La Rocha.

"But, I am here to offer her the opportunity of a lifetime!" he squeaked. Madam scowled. He whipped out his and Lucy Duff-Gordon's calling cards and gave one each to the teacher and the beautiful, willowy girl.

The teacher continued to scowl. The girl, Maria something or other, Gaston reported, nodded cooly and said, "Merci, Monsieur," and tucked the cards into her pocket.

"What is her name?" Lady Duff-Gordon asked her wheezing companion.

"I said, Maria something."

"No last name? You are slipping, Gaston. You are getting old."

"She will call."

"How do you know?"

"Because she has that look in her eye."

Maria squirmed in her seat at the dinner table. Her parents argued over whether or not Maria should be allowed to contact this Lucy Duff-Gordon person.

"It doesn't matter what you say, Papá," Maria commented when she could get a word in.

Her battling parents looked at her. "What do you mean, girl?" her stern maman asked, right before her papá grunted and said, "Let her call. There is nothing for her here."

"She is engaged!"

"Maman, I told you, I will not marry Anton Grabovski. You waste your time."

"You will do as we say."

"Let her go, Alene. Maybe nothing will come of it, and it will give her something to do besides brood. The marriage is not for three years."

"It still doesn't matter, Papá."

Her father looked at her impatiently.

"I am eighteen in one month. It is 1912. You cannot make

me marry against my will. Besides, that boy, Anton, is a 15 year-old, pimply-face cretin, with only a big pocketbook to recommend him. He's stupid. He can't even spell our last name. He thinks the Crimea is a primary color! You should be ashamed to have sold me to him."

And with that, Maria left the table and prepared to go to Paris in one month's time, because she knew who Lucy Duff-Gordon was, even if her bankrupt aristocratic parents did not.

Paris
Maria Pelletier Makes Up Her Mind

It took Maria Pelletier no time at all to make up her mind. Her parents didn't know her bags were packed and stashed under the bed for the two weeks since she'd been home from Paris.

And what they also didn't know was, on that excursion with La Rocha and the other girls, their hotel was just around the corner from the Saint-Michel. When all were bedded down, Madame tucked safely in the bar with an old friend and a bottle of cognac, Maria slipped out a side door and ran to the lobby of the imposing Saint-Michel. She presented Monsieur Gaston LeFevre's card to the Concierge. "Please tell Monsieur LeFevre that Maria Pelletier is calling."

There, after a brief tete a tete with the purpled Gaston, she threw her arms in the air with joy. If she'd had on a hat, she would have tossed it! Paris!

Out of the frying pan, into the fire.

Maria wasn't in Paris a month (without that sheep dog, La Rocha) before she fell in love. Well, at least the idea of love. He was handsome. He was lavish with money. He taught her about love. Ah, he taught her about rapture. He was a bit older, it's true, but what girl wouldn't want an older, experienced lover to teach her the beautiful way of it? Just ask her not-born-yet granddaughter, Stevie.

Every day, after grueling hours of calisthenics and stretching and beauty treatments and walking endlessly up and down ramps with a variety of props including a dictionary balanced on her head to improve her posture, she met her lover at his apartment for a tryst. Later, at the flat she shared with the other Duff-Gordon mannequins-to-be, Maria collapsed into bed and planned her future.

Marcel would help her with her new career, marry her, be with her forever. She'll have money to do as she pleases. She can make art. *And not get stuck in some crumbly old country manor just to bail out my parents' ruin.*

Yes, she thought. *I left home for this.*

Maria pined for Marcel on weekends, when he was away "on business." Her face suffered for the tears and her figure compromised by the secret compensatory pints of ice cream eaten in the dark. Her coach shamed Maria to change her ways: she would never make it to New York if she kept this up.

"But, I love him," Maria said.

"Bah!" (same meaning, any language) retorted her coach.

One night, after the drama died down over the sinking of the Titanic, after they celebrated the gutsy and shall we say pushy survival of Lady Duff-Gordon (it was rumored she shoved someone of lesser significance out of the way as she and her companions, including her little dog, Fifi, and the devoted Gaston, climbed into the one of the lifeboats), most everyone in the company had a drink or took a pill and crashed into bed. Maria used the key to her lover's apartment, to lie in the rumpled bed and nuzzle into his scent for comfort. Although the apartment was off-limits when he was away, she knew he wouldn't mind, this once. "I missed you so, Marcel," she planned to say. "I was so afraid for Madame Lucile and so many died!" She imagined his arms around her.

What she saw when she opened the door was worse than if she had seen him buck naked having sex with a sunflower on the dining room table. Marcel was sitting on the sofa, laughing, with a woman obviously his wife! Their children played with the puppy on the floor. The woman rested her hand on his thigh. His arm lay on the back of the sofa, hand on her lovely shoulder.

He looked up into Maria's hurt and furious and crushed eyes.

She turned away and, yes, almost immediately, took the Mauretania to the States to begin her career.

Our Maria had done something foolish, but our Maria was no fool. And she was becoming quite good at making up her mind.

Spring 1922
New York, New York
Ticket to Freedom

*T*his was my ticket to freedom, to life, *she thought,* and now, ten years later, I am its slave.

Maria Pelletier sat in her shared flat in the New York Young Ladies Club, looking out the window at the building next door. It was so close, she could see into her neighbor's living room. She didn't know her name, but she knew this woman "entertained" several different men; she knew that one man drank martinis, the other Manhattans, and the third, beer. She saw the woman walk in and out of the kitchen door, or disappear down the hall, alone or with one, or the other, or the other man. Fortunately, Maria could not see into the bedroom.

Maria was tired of this. She would like to see the sun rise. Or set. She would like to see the sun, period. She would like to bask in sun.

Maria's days began before the sun appeared in the sky. Her role as a principal model at the Lucile Salon wrapped her up in flowing silks and satins, velvets and fringe and elegant embroidery, all the livelong day. When she wasn't being pinned into outfits for the latest photo shoot, or gliding down runways in velvet-trained gowns, or turning her lovely profile this way or that in this or the other straw hat of the day, she exercised in the indoor pool or walked up and down flights of stairs with weights in her hands and rocks tied in socks around her ankles.

I am tired of tuna and cucumbers for lunch, poached chicken for dinner.

This night, she sat alone in her room with a smuggled bag of powdered donuts, remembering the pâtisserie in her home town.

She rubbed the confectioner's sugar between her fingers, sniffed the donut for that dusty sweetness, longed for a cup of dark roast coffee.

Her young friend, Katherine, one of Lucile's design interns, invited her to a Spring weekend in Hudson, Ohio—where she planned to visit her betrothed, a professor at Case Western Reserve. Katherine's parents didn't want the 20-year-old to go solo. Maria laughed at that notion—like she would be any kind of chaperone. *But, I weel go. I weel go into the salon tomorrow and tell Monsieur Gaston I need a weekend off. What a good idea.*

Gaston had been wrong about Maria Pelletier. What he took for "that look" ten years go on the street in Paris, was actually just desperation. Maria would have done anything— pick cotton, drive a truck, jump out of an airplane—if it would release her from her parents' grim plan. It's not like she spent her whole young life imagining herself as a model in New York and Paris. Maria had other plans.

You might wonder what Maria did with her nights in New York, after her own first affair died the moment she appeared unannounced at her lover's door. Nights were not about men. Maria was finished with men. Her heart would be broken only once.

She did admit, however, that if she were ever going to be discussing first time sex with her as yet unborn granddaughters, she had no regrets. She was sorry it ended the way it did, because croissants and espresso in bed in the mornings with Marcel after a night full of passion made for bittersweet memories, when she remembered he was a liar and a cheat.

Although Maria was a free spirit, she was no flapper, and kept herself to herself. To sooth her creative drive, Maria made afghans. No ordinary blankets, but wondrous works of art. She ripped discarded gold lamé fabric into strips and knitted them into her creations. Beads and baubles, embroidered flowers, ribbons, sequins and bits of glitz she found on the showroom floor, now stored in small bowls and baskets. Lucile's trash was Maria's treasure.

Maria sold her creations, saved her money and bought a sewing machine, setting it up in the corner of her bedroom. She left little room to walk: fabric sprawled over the chairs, rolled into neat bolts, or folded and stacked, and piles of loose yarn spilled over baskets.

Around 8 o'clock every night, Maria came into the apartment from the salon and flopped on the bed. Part of her just wanted to sleep. But the other part, the creative urge that blew her out of the gentrified but bankrupt lives of her parents and into the world she now lived, kept her alert and awake until midnight, long after her roommates, babbling about the New York nightlife, were asleep.

After a ten or fifteen minute rest, Maria's creations called to her, urging her fingers to touch their smooth surfaces, feast her eyes on the silky greens, velvety maroons, glittering crystal beads. Maria spent the next few hours piecing together her fantastic creations.

And counting her money.

Stevie's Red Book
Mama Maria tells me
her story

My grandmother, all Frenchified down to her pink garter-belt, told me her story. Wowie zow. I know things about her now that no one else knows. Even Poppy.

Can I write this down? I guess not. As a recorder of life, there are things that must not be written.

She said she wanted me to know her truth; that sex, especially the first time, was different for everyone.

She said, "Picasso was right."

I'm glad I asked, though she didn't give me enough details. I wonder how long I'll have to wait until I get down to the nitty gritty. Who will tell me?

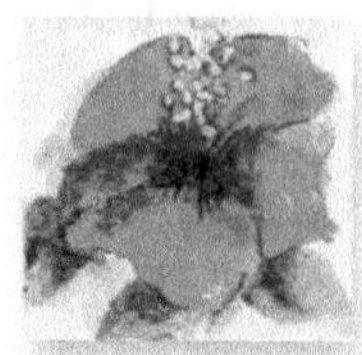

Meanwhile, in London
Nana & Jo Discuss Their IT

After Fox and Deke's wedding in January, Nana and Jo had arrived in London just as the school term began and life resumed. No time to consider the implications of a Magic Wand full of diamonds (Jo stashed it in a safety deposit box), not to mention the Green Chair and whatever its secret.

Finally in May, they met in a tea room near Grand Mamá Charlotte's for a private conversation.

Their current debate: how much to tell Lady Charlotte. Jo voted to tell her everything so they could just go to the house and pull the green chair apart to find the next clue to her father's mysterious past and the answer to the riddle in the poem. Nana's was the clandestine, and perhaps more dignified approach: tell Charlotte nothing and get in and out of the green chair without her knowledge.

Jo rolled her eyes, à la cousin Tate, to show her disdain.

"Why should we sneak around, Mum? Why shouldn't Grand Mamá Charlotte know the truth? I'll bet she'd be happy to put this mystery to bed. All this has been kept from her forever. If I were Grand Mamá, and all the men were dead, I'd want to know why."

"I just don't want to upset her, Jolene. She's been through enough and I am feeling protective."

"Pish," said her daughter. "You don't want her stirred up over this because you're about to lay down the I've-got-a-boyfriend card."

"What? What makes you say that?" Nana asked behind a blush.

"Mum. Don't take me for an idjit. I can read your mind. And now I've met Will, well, I think you should just get on with it. He's a catch. The opposite of Dad. Way lower maintenance. And he sings!"

"OK, let's not change the subject."

"You have to talk about it sometime."

"I know. We will. Just, let's make a plan for this, and maybe it will help me put the whole thing to rest, so I can get on with my life. Because, so far, Chuck still screws with me from the grave. This key around my neck? I want to fit it into something and have the demons stop following me and then I want to go off and have a beautiful life."

"Demons?"

"Oh. I don't know. Your father's voice. Lots of voices."

Pause. Jo cocked her head.

"Humming?" asked Jo.

Her mother looked at her. "Yes, actually."

"And the smell of gin?"

Nana nodded.

"Do you have that, too?" Nana asked.

"I did. I performed a ritual. He's quieter. He has things on his mind. It's like, he's not done here yet. You need a ritual, Mum. To help put him to rest."

"I'm not much for rituals, Jolene."

"Oh no? You don't think this whole key thing is anything but a ritual? I'll bet when you find the lock that fits the key, the voices will go away."

"That's what I said to my sisters."

"It'll help Dad rest, I think."

Nan heard Will's voice, "It is time, my darling, to chirp or get off the twig."

Nana Huffington and Jo Huff Crack the Code

"All right, you win, Jolene," Nana said to her daughter, a few days later in the same tearoom. Jo Huff had shed her school uniform that Saturday for a Pierre Cardin knock-off space suit: gold-belted aubergine tunic, gold lamé tights and black knee-high go go boots.

The gold made her mother's teeth itch, but she didn't say anything. Jo had her artistic expression going. No use getting into an argument over that! There were other things to consider today.

"Oh, good, I win. What am I winning, Mum? Must be important. You're wearing black."

"What?"

"Black is your power color. Red would be more effective. You look good in red."

Nana checked to see if anyone listened to this conversation. No one paid them any mind. She looked down at her clothes: black turtleneck, black slacks, black belt, black loafers. She shook her head. She gave her daughter's outfit the once over. She'd stick with black.

"You win, we'll tell your Grand Mamá Charlotte about the curse or whatever it is. We'll tell her everything. It would be insulting to leave her out of it, like she's a child, which she surely is not. And, I don't want to sneak around. I think I'd feel like a thief.

"And, I'm sorry I argued about it."

Jo stared at her mother. Nana Huffington was not known for admitting she was wrong, much less apologizing. Nana's way in the world was to ignore impending danger or drama, thereby making it bigger than life in the end. She was never one for introspection.

Jo said, "Who are you and what have you done with my mum?"

Nana laughed. "It's me alright. But, I have do a caveat, since I still have reservations about exposing all this to a 75-year-old widow who has also outlived her sons and will soon face living alone again. So, yes, this is important, and yes, you were right about my getting ready to bring Will to her attention. It's time. But, I wasn't joking about not riling her up."

"Mum, honestly? I think she'll be delighted."

Nana scoffed.

"No, really. Grand Mamá is bored."

The Green Chair
for Jo

Behind the green chair, there's a wish and a prayer
There's a song to be sung, and bells to be rung
If you are smart and open your heart
The news will be good all over the 'hood

I'll sing you my songs all the day long
But you've never heard such encouraging words
I'll be there for you in all that you do
It's incredible, wonderful, fabulous news

So take heart my girl, though I'm in the next world
You're free from now on, now that I'm gone
The spell is lifted, to you this is gifted
The darkness is over, and you are in clover

Babblety-bee Babblety-boo,
I wrote this silly poem for you
It means nothing now I know but soon,
Bibblety babblety boo

Nana held the poem in one hand. With the other, she fingered the key on the long chain around her neck. She felt like an idiot, reading the poem (which made about as much sense as chocolate and clams on a pizza). Out loud, no less. Not to mention telling Lady Charlotte about this spell in which she, Nana, did not believe. But, Chuck had. And Jolene, who stood near the fireplace fidgeting, (*God in Heaven, what is she wearing? Pink leather?*) wanted to know her father's story. And Will said he would believe anything if it got Nana moving their plans forward.

Lady Charlotte's substantial rump happened to be on the Green Chair. She squirmed a little, rustling her red silk slip. She put her hands on the arms of the chair, as if she might be propelled out of it at any moment. She felt the perspiration on the palms of her hands and lifted them off the antimacassars, always careful of the velvet. She took a paper napkin from the tea tray on the coffee table in front of her and rolled it between the palms of her hands, then folded it neatly and set it on the table beside the tray.

Charlotte Huffington had long known there was more to the Huffington male madness than met the eye. Her husband, the late Lord Charles, lips loosened by whiskey, referred often to family secrets and hidden treasures. And, he once tossed something in the desk drawer, locked it and, seeing her at the open door, looked guilty, like a straying husband. But, she knew he didn't have affairs. He was too afraid of everything to pull that off.

Nana continued, "So, since there is nothing behind the chair, we think there might be something *in* the chair itself.

Something that explains the poem. And maybe the key."

Nana babbled from nerves and excitement. Bibblety babblety boo. She was a little afraid of what Lady Charlotte would think of all this. Would she roll her eyes and say, "You silly girls, what nonsense"? Would she be upset? Dramatic? Nana didn't think so. But she didn't expect this.

Lady Charlotte laughed. She laughed so hard it made her cry, and once her tears began to flow, she laughed and cried with British gusto. Jo and Nana patted her hand, while Nana gave her daughter a meaningful look that said, "See? We've upset her."

Charlotte recovered in five minutes. *Gather your wits, woman*, she mumbled to herself.

"What a relief!" she said out loud, wiping her eyes. "Now I understand why he bothers me so."

Jo looked at her mother and said to her grandmother, "Grand Mamá, what do you mean? Who bothers you?"

"Oh, Your father. Young Charles. He sits in this chair. I usually don't sit here. I don't like it, never have, but he likes to sit here. It's the only reason I keep it. His father used to appear here, too, but he doesn't come anymore. Charles makes all kinds of noises and gestures, like he is trying to tell me something. I know when he's there. The chair creaks."

Nana and Jo shared a look.

"Do you hear his voice, Grand Mamá?"

"Oh, yes, but he doesn't really say anything. A lot of Ta Das and Oomp-pa-pas, but no words. Humming, sometimes. And he smells strange, like a Christmas tree. Like juniper."

Jo giggled. "Like a Martini?"

"Why, yes. That's it! How do you know this? Are you saying you hear him, too?" Charlotte looked from mother to daughter and back again. They filled her in on their own experiences.

In a few minutes, Charlotte rose from the chair. She went to the pantry, lifted the little tool box off the bottom shelf and brought it to the parlor. She took out scissors, pliers and a little screw driver. She handed them to Jolene and said, "Since the poem was addressed to you, and it seems to concern you more than anyone, do whatever needs to be done to the green chair."

Jo smiled at her mother, who nodded. "Just be careful," Nana said.

"Oh, tear the blasted thing apart if you have to, I don't care," Charlotte said. "After this, we can throw the ugly thing out."

Lady Charlotte looked around the drawing room and chose the Queen Anne next to the fireplace, with its polished cherry wood back, arms and legs and red brocade seat cover. Lord Charles never did let her re-upholster that green chair! *Well, it can go, now!*

Jo circled the chair, pondering its contents. She assumed the back came off, but wanted to get to know the chair first. Firm, upright wingback, wings like a butterfly, slightly tipped outward from the back of the chair. Unworn deep green velvet, fat, firm cushion.

She moved 'round to the back: straight, well padded, tight seams. It didn't look like a trick chair—just a chair. *If something's in it, it's well disguised,* she thought. *You'd really have to know it was there to find it.*

She crouched down. No seams, just one solid piece of fabric from top to bottom. She put her hand at the top, slowly gliding her hand down the back of the chair, feeling from right to left, left to right as she moved toward the bottom, one inch at a time. Nana and Charlotte watched, quiet as library mice.

Slowly, side to side, left to right, right to left. Her hands moved in rhythmic motion. Just at the bottom, it felt different. Extra padding here. Push in, push in, Ohh, a tiny snap. Six tiny snaps. Putting her small fingers along the edge of the chair now, she found an opening between the snaps, less than an inch. She gently pulled and the snaps gave way, widening the opening, revealing part of the wood frame of the chair. Oh, not part of the chair. She could see now, the chair had been altered to accommodate a box about 8 inches wide and two inches high. It slid under the cushion on little slats. Jo pulled open a few more snaps, wiggled the screw driver into a side and pried the old box out.

Jo looked at her mother.

Nana, expelling her held breath, could barely get the words out. She handed Jo the key and whispered, "That must be it."

Jolene looked the box over and said, "No, Mum. No lock."

Mother and grandmother sentries sat still. Jo opened the little wooden box. The smell of naphthaline made Jo hold the box away from her nose. She set it down on the rug in front of her, took out and set aside the single mothball. Before going further, she looked at her mother, and then her grandmother. She raised her eyebrows, like, "Ok, here we go!" And in that moment, under all that red mop of coiling hair, she looked just like Chuck.

Jo pulled out a rolled paper tied with a ribbon and a piece of ancient-looking, burn-scarred fabric. Next a fragment of thin porcelain, perhaps from a saucer, an old coin, an oil painter's brush and a ring engraved on the inside—RFH 1854. As Jo removed items from the box, she set them carefully on the rug. When she handled the small ivory hairbrush, she shuddered. After she took out a cuff link and a tarnished brass button, she found a thick, folded piece of paper: an old map with a circle drawn around a place called Uffa's Town, in West Berkshire, where the old family estate had been. Now maybe she'll find out why it had been abandoned.

Jo picked up the piece of rolled paper and untied the ribbon. When she saw her father's handwriting, she started to cry.

Nana was crying too, Charlotte, trying not to. Nana said, "I've seen that brush."

Charlotte replied, "Given to Charles at his christening. I forget from whom."

Jo did not hear them. Reading the letter from her father took all her attention.

Dear Jolene,

If you are reading this, I am gone to the Creator and you have found a clue to bring you closer to our family Truth. I commend your finding the hiding place in the Green Chair, on whose cushion I have placed my derriere for many hours in contemplation of this tragic circumstance.

The spell is many generations old. It is and has been such a deep family secret that you are the first female of the line to know of it. Actually, you are the first female of the line since the curse was cursed, or the spell was spoken, which is the point.

It began with a Huffington and a woman in the late 18th century, on the Huffington farm, seven generations ago. This woman hated him and our family and, in the short version for the purpose of this letter and your immediate relief, used herbs and simples to curse the family name of Huffington. A spell of failure and madness on the men. I was no exception. The curse ends with me, last of the male Huffingtons. Thus, the suggested new name of Jo Huff. It's a spell breaker, don't you think?

How does one cope with a curse? Deny it? Believe it? Ignore it? It is truly not ignorable. I have moments of clear sight, as now, when I write to you. I call it the Bright Time. But for me the curse has made me into two distinct people—and the unclear side, the mad side, the Dark Time, will take me down. Which is when you will read this letter.

If you want to know more, there is a leather book in this flat somewhere, scribbled in by various Huffingtons during their lifetimes. "As things continue

*to demolish my life, I find I must keep notes." Those
are the first words in the book, written by the hand of
the original cursed Huffington.*

*By the time you read this, the leather book may be in
a box. Once it was in the library, hidden in plain sight.
Not sure, now. It will tell you much about the lives,
and deaths, of the Huffington males, as well as the
items in the box.*

*I will tell you this: the witch died in prison, for all the
good it did the Huffingtons.*

The key will open the book.

With all love, your father

Charles Wayland Huffington
1955 London

I wish you love and complete peace.

And on a separate paper scrap, tucked inside the letter, Jo
Huff found this:

1960

*On the occasion of my death, I leave to Jolene
Huffington my conductor's baton, with an investment
made on her behalf during a Bright Time a few years
ago.*

Signed,

Charles Wayland Huffington

Grand Mamá Charlotte's Flat
London
Three Women

Jo Huff wore dark red Chinese silk pajamas embroidered with pink and yellow roses. Her new buddy, Rollie, encouraged her to stop thinking about clashing hair and wear whatever she wanted. Her hair was "the bees knees," he said. Toes warmed in fluffy bunny-nose slippers, she sat on the floor in her grandfather's library amid a stack of small boxes pulled from the lower bookshelves.

Grand Mamá, sans corset, in flannel pajamas and red velvet scuffs, her fluffy white hair aglow with purpose, pulled a leather bin out of the closet.

Nana, still in creased slacks (black, Jo noticed) and sweater set (grey, yawn) from her evening out, sat at the desk, rifling around in the drawers.

"This looks promising," Grand Mamá Charlotte grunted as she lifted the bin onto the desk.

The place was in shambles, as if ransacked by the Mafia or the CIA: drawers left open, papers spilling out, stacks of books on the floor.

Earlier that evening, while Nana and her boyfriend wooed each other over Amber Ale and steak pie in the Bull's Eye Tavern, Jo and Grand Mamá Charlotte considered the morning's events. Jo's delicious dinner (Aubergines stuffed with chopped veggies, bread crumbs and Parmesan cheese and a composed salad with sections of mandarin orange, slivered almonds and bits of smoked duck) was swiftly consumed while they talked and talked: about Charles, his up and down life, the curse, family secrets. They didn't turn on the telly, or listen to the radio. They sat at the dining room table and talked.

They got into their pajamas, reconvened in the library and picked up the conversation. Jo listened to her grandmother's stories of her small and calm life in the country, before Lord Charles, and her life in town, after, with one drama after another.

"We never did visit the old estate in Uffa's Town. Lord Charles refused to go, saying, 'The past is past. Let it be.'"

"What do you suppose he did?" Jo asked. She didn't expect her grandmother to have the answer, but saying it out loud gave the story legs, made these people real, more than nameless ancestors, silent predecessors, holders of secrets. Jo wanted names. She wanted Truth, a capital T truth.

"What who did, dear?"

"The original Huffington man who caused a woman to curse him and his male heirs until there weren't any more."

"Yes, I see. Well, that's the next question, isn't it? Read me the poem again and the part in the letter about the leather book. Perhaps we'll find another clue."

"Grand Máma."

"What is it, Jo?"

"I thought I killed him."

"What? Killed who? Your father? How in the world?"

And so, Jo finally told someone (she never guessed it would be her grandmother) about the night her father died—his 2 am visit to Jo in her room at Sweet Farm, the dramatic speech about getting this conductor's job, his leave-taking, her letting him go. She let him go. And he drove off a bridge. She never forgave herself for letting him go.

She told her grandmother all about the imaginary box she created—full of his last words, "Don't tell, Jo," as well as her guilt and deep remorse. She described wrapping the imaginary box in imaginary music and cobwebs and wool and giving the whole enchilada to the sea, on the beach where he died. She told her about the owl feather, dropped into her hand out of the sky, about Old Joe and his cabin under Bixby Bridge and his gift, his keeping the magic wand for her because he knew she'd come sooner or later. She told her grandmother the whole story of how she really came upon the magic wand full of diamonds in the woods under Bixby Bridge.

"Finally," Jo said to her grandmother. "Finally I see that it wasn't my fault. It wasn't my letting him go that night, when I wasn't sure at all if he was drunk or sober, that led to his death. He might well have been stone cold sober, like he said. He was just, already, on his way out. It was only a matter of time. He was an incredibly restless person. It was like he suddenly said, 'Let's get on with it,' and left all the pain behind."

Of course, Charlotte was in tears when Jo finished this little litany of secrets stashed in an imaginary box in the sea.

And by the time Nana returned from her date (more about that later), the senior Lord Charles's ghostly library had been turned upside down. Jo and her grandmother were on a break, each with a cup of tea, a plate of biscuits and a tiny glass of sherry.

It took no time for Nana to be bitten by the same bug, the "find the blasted book and get on with our lives" bug. Soon, all the desk drawers were pulled out, uncovering a few mysterious items: a stack of yellowed papers marked "private" (which looked like a list of provisions in the case of an alien attack), a piece of toast about 30 years old, six Roman coins and her late father-in-law's loaded pistol, which she slid to the back of the drawer.

Charlotte dug through the leather bin. She looked over at Nana and asked, "How was your evening, dear Nana?" She didn't think Nana would tell her, but she had to ask. It was their ritual. (Charlotte: "How was your evening?" Nana: "Fine.")

Nana, startled out of a reverie, said, "It was fine." Charlotte shook her head. Jo gave her mother a glance full of unspoken words. Sometimes they communicated through waves and particles. Nana saw portent in the wide open eyes of her daughter.

"What?" Nana asked Jo. "What is it?"

"You may as well come clean, Mum. I told her."

"Told her what?"

"Told Grand Mamá all about William. She even knows who he is. She's heard him sing. It's all out now. I did it for you. You're welcome."

"Jolene Huffington! No!" Nana felt Charlotte's eyes on her. She turned her head, expecting the worst—disappointment, shock, anger. But, Charlotte was smiling.

"Oh, Charlotte, I…" Nana didn't know quite what to say, or how much Jolene had spilled—the whole jar of beans, or just one or two? *Oh, God. Now what am I going to have to explain? This is all just too much.*

Charlotte Huffington, unmasked now in every way—no make up, no corset, no hat, no jewels—felt alive for the first time in many years. The minute Nana finished reading the odd little poem that morning, Charlotte felt as if the dark had released the light. The weight of the drama, the drinking, the secrets, the deaths: it had been on her head for more years than that piece of toast lay in the drawer next to a loaded pistol.

"Nana, dear, give me more credit. Do you think I have been unaware of your comings and goings? You're silly to think I would resent your loving someone other than Charles. Besides dear, he's long dead, and he was a passel of trouble when alive.

"I want to hear all about your William. Of course, I'll want to meet him."

Jo beamed at her fabulous new grandmother! Yesterday she was laced up in a corset and tonight she's not only in flannel pajamas (true, she wore a sort of bra, but she'd kind of have to with those abundant bosoms, wouldn't she? *I'd want to strap them in a bit, if they were mine, and mine are big enough*), but she was talking to Jo and her mother as if they were true friends. Like she, Jo, was an adult and Nana, her mother, was someone Charlotte actually liked, not just put up with because of her son and granddaughter.

Three women who just this morning were on different planets: Jo, gnashing at the bit to dig up her ancestors' stories; Nana, worried about her mother-in-law, her secret boyfriend, her dead husband's dark family drama and a mysterious magic wand full of diamonds; and Lady Charlotte Huffington, bored silly by her book group, tea and the telly.

Chapter Five

July

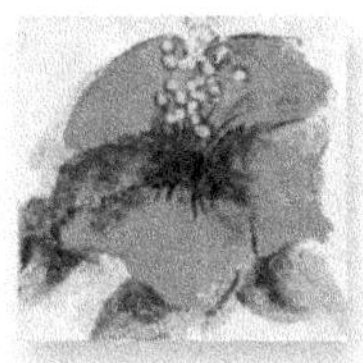

Dearest Steve and Tate,

I am sitting at the big desk amidst the rubble that was once my grand papa's library. The desk is pulled apart, and we have found all kinds of treasures and strange things, but not the book, which started the search.

After we pried open the green chair and opened the box full of tiny objects (you'd really dig it, Stevie— there are rings and maps and all kinds of stuff hundreds of years old), Grand Mamá and I talked and talked.

Grandmothers! I heard stories about Lord Charles and my dad's whacko brother, Rafe, who actually did hide in a munitions warehouse during the war, by the way. She said someone saw him peer out the small window in the door just before the building blew up. So, she knew he had been hiding, and she knew for sure he was dead, and not MIA, as she first heard.

I've never seen my grandmother so—light. She's all of a sudden…buoyant. You should have seen her in flannel jammies. Her white hair was electric, sticking out like your mom's, Tate, only not red. She practically threw her back out lifting boxes from cupboards trying to find the missing leather book, which we didn't. But, she was lit up like a Christmas tree, so happy to be free of the dark cloud over her family for, like, ever.

More later,

Love, Jo Huff

June 1964

From San Francisco to Salinas to Carmel

Beth Warner Arrives

Beth Warner changed her life by taking a three hour train ride from San Francisco to Salinas. It wasn't a snap decision, but when she heard of this opportunity, she knew it was hers. She did not look back.

Well, she did look back, in a way. Three hours on a train with no companion, not even a book to read, gave the light behind her closed eyelids the perfect opportunity for flashing vignettes of the last few years. Good and bad, personal and professional, she saw it all, neon, bigger than life, as if the screen behind her closed eyes projected the Saturday afternoon matinee and her life, the main attraction. It wasn't pretty, most of it. Not for the faint of heart.

She set aside her nurse's uniform for jeans and a t-shirt. She didn't think the whites would be necessary in Carmel Valley. When she met her ride, she knew her answer.

"Sorry to pick you up in the truck," Fox said, as she introduced herself and tossed Beth's bags in the back. "Fenn's bringing his mother home in his van and Jock and Maria are in Morro Bay with the Sweet Farm chariot so, here we are."

Beth laughed and looked dubiously into the bed of the pick up. "I don't mind," she said. "I've always wanted my bags to smell like pig poop." She blew her long straight bangs out of her eyes.

Fox turned to Beth and said, "It's chicken. And there *is* a tarp." Beth took in the redheaded Fox Wyman, and Fox Wyman examined the nurse. About the same size, they somehow seemed on equal ground. *What does that mean?* thought Fox. *Equal ground?*

Well, for one thing, from that moment by the back of the truck on a busy Saturday afternoon at the train station in Salinas, with a conversation that began with pig poop, two girls in jeans, Fox and Beth, felt as if they had known each other all their lives. By the time they drove into Fenn Cooper's driveway on El Camino Estrada, Fox blushed to think she had actually told someone within ten minutes of meeting that she intended to leave Sweet Farm.

It was right after Beth said, "Well, to be honest, I took this job with Fenn Cooper because I had to get out of the City for a while. Two break-ups and fifteen years in the ER took the steam out of my engine. I traded in Santa Clara Hospital for home care, at the moment in Carmel Valley. I'd rather watch over Fenn's mother than patch up one more bleeding street kid. I need a rest. From a lot of things."

Fox said, "Hm. I want to get out of *here* and go to the City."

Beth could tell by Fox's face, even in profile, there was more in the statement than a simple wish for new horizons. "Why?" she asked.

Beth noticed Fox's hands grip the wheel. Fox glanced at Beth and back to the road. "Honestly?" she asked. "The truth is, Beth, I don't love my husband."

"How long have you been married?"

"Six months," Fox said. That sounded ridiculous. "But it's complex." She was quiet for a moment. "See, my husband disappeared almost fourteen years ago. He resurfaced last fall and…well, it's a baffling tale, for sure."

As they arrived in Carmel Valley 40 minutes later, Beth knew the gist of Deke's story and Fox's thirteen years without him and had to agree.

As Fox opened the driver's side door at Fenn's, she said to Beth, "Dammit. I don't believe I told you all that about leaving Sweet Farm. Please don't speak of it to anyone. Tate surely doesn't know this, and well, she's another whole conversation. I didn't know myself until I just said it out loud."

"No, Fox, I won't tell. I want to hear the rest, though. It sounds like a dilly." She smiled.

"No doubt you will."

Imagine that. Fox has a friend.

June 1964
Is He Beautiful?

As they closed the doors on the truck, Fox said, "I suppose Fenn Cooper has filled you in about his mother?"

Beth threw the pack over her shoulder and picked up the bigger, now slightly chicken-y bag. She said, "Enough. He says she's a cranky old virago who needs help with her wigs." Both women laughed.

"Sounds like Fenn Cooper to me!" said Fox.

"I also know she is a…wow," she whispered. "Who is that beautiful man?"

Fox looked up. *Crapola.* She pursed her lips and said, "That's Deke Harley. My husband. He must be here to fix the gate." *Is he beautiful?* Fox's cheeks flushed with competing emotions: she twitched her lip, raised her eyebrows, looked at her new friend, and mumbled, "Huh!"

Deke met up with them at the path to Fenn's door. He put out his hand and said, "Hi, I'm Deke Harley." Beth smiled, put her hand in his and said, "Beth Warner. Really nice to meet you, Deke Harley."

Fox and Beth exchanged a glance. Beth noticed Fox's furrowed brow. Fox noticed Beth's dimple and laughed, even though she was suddenly confused. *Is he beautiful?*

Deke took Beth's big bag and led the way along the path. Fox fell in behind them, studying the backside of the new nurse: white blonde hair cut in shaggy disarray just below

148

the ears, straight bangs down to her dark eyes and lashes. An exotic beauty and perhaps Fox's own age. Her jeans fit well and Fox loved the leather lace-up sandals.

Beth turned around. Fox felt caught. She stepped back and looked down at her toes. Beth smiled and said, "Thanks for the ride, Fox."

June 1964
Saddle Mountain, Carmel Valley
Fox and Beth on the Path

"I feel a little funny, taking this time off."

"Mrs. Cooper doesn't need you hovering around her all the time, does she?"

"No. She needs her regular treatments and physical therapy, the cupping really helps, but you can't do that all the time, and the housekeeper will be there soon to bring her tea and tissues and wig spray and whatnot, so, no. There is no need to hover."

Fox smiled at the "whatnot." Such a Wyman word.

"And Fenn's there, right?"

"Yes."

"He's not paying you much, is he?"

"No, not really," Beth laughed.

"Then don't worry about it. Fenn needs you. No one has you on a time clock. Besides, it's 6 in the morning and I'll bet the old lady is sound asleep."

Beth laughed out loud.

Their booted feet took them up the path to the March of Trees along the Saddle Mountain ridge. Fox wanted to share the view with her friend. She also wanted to share the dream—Deke's dream: her, beckoning to him; him, stuck in molasses, yelling out to her with no words; her, humming, turning into a baby; his description of her slipping away into the March of Trees, getting smaller and smaller until she vanished into a dot on the landscape. And he didn't even know it was Fox. He just saw "a red girl." So sad.

"It's so hard to talk about. Everyone wishes I could pick up where we left off. They don't GET that we are two different people. Thirteen year is a long time."

Beth asked, "Did you ever love him?"

"Oh, God, Beth. Did I ever love him? He was the sun and the moon and the stars." Fox told her about their beginnings: the secret months of bliss in the bunkhouse, the moonlight on Deke's face, the tangled sheets and long talks in the dark.

"I said to Deke once, early on, 'We're like magnets.' That was the first thing he remembered about me when he woke up from the…the, you know, amnesia. He says he felt like a zombie, except he couldn't even articulate what a zombie was supposed to feel like. So, no, he's not the same person, nor am I.

"I feel awful about it, really. Why can't I love him? Why can't I be big-hearted and take him in, nurse him back to health, make him my project, at least. Try to love him, just a little? Or even pretend I love him? Why is that? Am I that hard? Am I cold and unfeeling, just because I want to love the person I'm with? I've been alone 13 years. Missing him. Waiting for him. And now? Sometimes I…I just don't know."

Fox stopped walking and looked at Beth. They had walked halfway up the mountain.

Beth said, "Are you asking my opinion? My advice? Because

if you are, I will tell you what I think about relationships. It's just an idea."

"Oh, do!"

"As a scientist, which I am in my heart of hearts, I see relationships as exchanges of energy. Sometimes we exchange energy with someone who feels the same way we do: loving a sunset, or listening to Bach—I don't know—just someone with whom you feel a kinship. Someone who is as weird as you are. One lover of mine said we vibrated at the same frequency. I liked that. But then, one day, for reasons I won't go into now, we stopped vibrating at the same frequency. Everything changed. And we weren't in love any more. There was love. But we weren't *in* love. Do you see?"

"Yes…"

"What I mean, Fox, is that people do change. Even without a trauma to the head. Frequencies change. Priorities evolve as we grow and then, those things change the person. Sometimes people grow together, commit to the frequency, and stay together for life. But I don't know much about that— at least, not yet.

"So, that's my view as a scientist. I know it's pretty 'out there,' but, it's funny, as a more spiritual concept, I would say exactly the same thing.

"I can't say if you should leave your husband, or give you all the reasons you should stay and suck it up. But if I speak from my heart, I can say a woman has a right to be happy. You are not happy at all."

June 1964

Steve's Little Red Book

The Truth

Jo Huff is here for a month. The other day, the three of us cousins walked up Ocean Avenue in downtown Carmel.

Jo wanted to go into this new shop near San Carlos Street called Adam Fox to buy a gadget for Poppy's birthday, which was fine, but I couldn't get the name out of my head—Adam Fox. It made me laugh. I got the hysterical giggles and wouldn't explain, I just kept laughing and saying, Adam Fox, Adam Fox, so Tate and Jo rolled their eyes and made me stay outside to get my giggles under control.

I focused my eyes on a tree so when they came back, I was myself again. Jo said, "Let's get together in the Hobbit and talk about what's happened this year. No biggie-wow-wow revelations, or big Truths, just about our lives. I know I have stuff to talk about."

I said I did, too (I wanted to tell her more about the Farley kiss thing, still not ever planning to talk about the Adam/Deke Harley thing), but I could see Tate was dubious. Still, she didn't say no.

153

We planned a day, which was today.

I probably should have put the kibosh on it, could have been more sensitive to Tate's state of mind (reference Resolution #6), but I took for granted she would say no if she didn't want to bare her soul today. I gave her more credit for the word NO than I should have.

Our three grown selves squashed together in the Hobbit House Middle, in our faded yellow circle. (The tree house will always be our place, no matter how big we get).

Jo told us all about the new developments in the Mystery. It's so big and amazing, I asked her to write about it before she lost the thread. She said she would.

Then, for a few minutes, she had us (or at least, me) in stitches with details about her first not-kiss. Jo got all dolled up for this Rollie, planned the whole thing down to her checkered tights and the moment of lips meeting lips (which would take place in the theatre after he picked up her hand and kissed her palm, like any good prince) and Rollie turned out to be gay. "A friend of Dorothy's," he said, like she was supposed to know what that meant.

She said they are good friends now, but at the time she turned pink in her orange Mary Quant dress. Rollie came the next week on Sunday and took her to Piccadilly, where they ogled the same men and had Beef Pasties and butterscotch milkshakes.

Her first not-kiss turned out to be a lovely new friend. I am still on the outs with Farley. Tate is on the outs with the world, and Jo just did not get it. To fill in the gap of silence after Jo's hilarious story, I described my evening at the Salinas High Sock Hop. I was just getting to the part where I yelled at Farley to take me home, when Tate burst into a flood of tears.

Immediately sorry (of course it was my fault) I put my arm around her. Jo was speechless. I realized no one had told her about Tate's prom night, and I was suddenly in the middle of our Middle, our Switzerland, our safe space, the place where our secrets are safe, feeling guilty, weird and not safe at all.

Jo gave me a look, like, "What did I do?" I responded with silent gestures meaning, "Nothing! It's not you!" and then asked her to get a teapot refill from Rita, which she happily did.

I held onto Tate and rocked her, like I used to when she missed her dad. I mumbled platitudinous garbage like, "Shh, it'll be all right," and "It's OK, Tatie. It's OK." But I was down to the bottom of my bag of comforts, and clueless. Although I did think it was pretty amazing that, like it or not, want it or not, we'd all been thinking about kissing.

Before Jo returned from the Tea Room, Tate made an excuse and scrambled out of the Hobbit to go to her room. She said, "I'm sorry" about 100 times, and 100 times, I said, "It's not your fault."

I thought the right thing to do was to fill Jo in on the details, so this wouldn't happen again. And, against all Girl Cousin Club rules, I did the unthinkable—I broke the "anything that happens in the Hobbit stays in the Hobbit" agreement. I told Deke and Fox what happened and said, "My cousin needs help."

June 1964
Berkeley California
Under the Covers
Letter from Farley to Stevie

Dear Stevie,

Lights are out in the dorm. I am under the covers, writing by spelunker's spotlight strapped to my head so as not to disturb my roommate, John Lauderdale, who sleeps like the dead, so I don't know why I bother. John is a surfer from Brentwood, a new breed of boy: tan, blond and perpetually dressed in Hawaiian shirts, shorts and flip flops. He is depressed by the unwelcoming temperature (freezing) of the San Francisco Bay—spoiled kid from southern California beaches.

Stevie, I won't bore you with all the details of my daily life in dorm and classroom, but I'll just say, it smells like boys' socks in the dorm, rancid cooking oil and cleanser in the dining hall, unmentionable things in the bathrooms and chalk and sweat in the classrooms, just like always. Boys should not be let loose on the land at our age, proven by the mess, noise and general complications of life among them in close quarters. And it's noisy.

My days are crammed full of books, papers, and research, Judges Swann and Simpson in league to keep me so busy I barely have time to breath and eat, much less drink and party my way through college.

Steve, I am only going to say this once, and then my letters will be newsy and full of campus gossip and lofty thoughts, I promise. I just have to get off my chest some things bothering me lately, you probably know what they are.

First, I am truly sorry I caught you off guard and kissed you. Oh, you know I am not sorry it happened, I am just sorry you didn't like it. I was so sure you would.

Second, even though I liked it, if I could erase it from the slate, I would. Your friendship has been the best thing in my life to date, and I wouldn't do anything to harm that.

So, third, please accept my apology for being a dunderhead and not reading you right at all.

Your friendship, promised five years ago forever (with an exchange of bookmarks, if you'll remember—your green tiger with a tassel for my red leather stamped with FJS in gold) is more important than a mere sharing of kisses. One can always get kissed. But one cannot always find true friendship. I do love you, and if "as a friend" is where it's at, I'll take it.

I'll assume we are still friends and just move on to say I have received the invitation to your big Trio birthday party in the fall and I am glad you, or maybe your Aunt Fox, invited me. I will certainly be there, although I hope to see you before that.

Thank you for coming to my graduation ceremony. I have to say you looked as uncomfortable in that dress as I felt in my cap and gown but, is it OK to say? You looked beautiful.

Thank Tate for coming (it was nice of her to brave the crowd—I know she's kinda fragile), and for the canvas tote bag. It's come in handy already.

Write back and tell me the Sweet Farm news.

Sincerely,

Farley Simpson

Future esq.

July 1964

Dear Farley,

Thanks for your letter. I will try to forget it happened, but you don't just sweep those things under the rug and then pretend they are not there. It's bumpy. I worry you have done irreparable damage to a once great friendship, but I don't know.

It's easier to write than talk about it, so maybe I can work this out on paper, with you listening, from afar.

First, the whole you know who/Perfect Stranger thing? freaked me out about getting kissed at all. I thought I had that one handled, and look at the mess. As you said, I could have been dead in a motel room. Or worse, every member of my family would have definitely found out. Perfect Stranger, Interrupted!

So, I thought, no kissing for a long time. Maybe I'm too young to be kissed, although I know girls who have been making out with boys since they were twelve. I just want it to be on my terms, is all. That seems fair to me. No surprises. That's another place where you messed up. I hate surprises.

See, when we're not kissing, or worried about kissing, we talk. Perfect. I can tell you everything. And I always know you're there. But the kissing thing? Makes me want to hide in the closet and come out when I'm old, at least 30. Guess I'm just not ready after all.

After saying all that, at least you didn't spike the punch.

Stay my friend, Farley. I don't think we're meant to be kissing.

Sweet Farm News:

No dramas at the moment, amazing, I know. There is progress with Jo and the mysteries about her dad. I'll tell you all about it when you're here, but when Jo left London last week, Lady Charlotte was still digging through all the ancestral loot for the leather book that will tell all. As they say in the news, Film at 11. (In case you're not hip, that means, details later.)

As you could see at your graduation, Tate is better, but, pretty nervous around boys in general, even you.

She's seeing a shrink, which is good. I never thought I'd say that. I'm not even sure what shrinks do. But, she needs someone besides me to talk to, someone who might have advice other than, "Go thrash those boys. I'll help you." She shouldn't take advice from me.

Mama Maria and Poppy are on their Alaskan Cruise, celebrating her 70th and his 80th birthdays, eating Shrimp and Crab Louis and playing shuffleboard or whatever people do on Alaskan cruises when they aren't looking at icebergs and igloos and fishing for 30 pound salmon. So, that lowers my family count to 8 here at the farm. They'll be home at the end of the month. 10.

There is momentum building around this Trio Party. We have over 100 people coming to the "main event," which is Saturday BBQ, behind the barn: big tent, caterers, band. Tate is supposed to sing and play her guitar, but she's freaked out about it now. She says all those people know about That Night, and she's embarrassed. I hope she plays. Deke and Fáno are building a little stage.

The illustrious Grand Mamá Charlotte is coming, and Will Cameron, too, Aunt Nana's mystery lover. All nooks and crannies at Sweet Farm will be occupied and then some. Cousin André can't make it from the lavender fields in France, just as well. No one likes him. Deke's mother, Rebecca, will be here, too.

And, Deke Harley. Can you believe he was ever gone or missing?

Film at 11, Steve

Revelation Tree

Fox, extricating herself from the straight jacket called "sleep," rolled out of the crowded bed (in Fox's world, one other person was a crowd, especially if the crowd = Deke) and into her slippers. It was 5am and the crowd in question lay on his back conked out, completely still.

Once, my mornings were full of longing: for love, for relating, for Deke, for what was. Now, I want none of that, and want only to be alone. Mornings now are best spent walking. Hm. The only time I am alone, and yet, now I have invited Beth to walk with me. Now, why is that?

Because, being with her is like being alone, only better.

Oh, brother. How would I explain that to Deke, to my mother, to Beth? How do I say I have never felt so completely comfortable? That a girlfriend has given me more direct understanding and empathy than any human to date?

It must be me. Maybe I am the one who needs a shrink. I am given my every dream, the return of my Deke, and it is not enough. It is so not enough, that I if I believe God answered a prayer, then I also believe She has a sense of humor. Certainly a sense of irony.

While thus ruminating, Fox stripped off her flannels and pulled on grey sweats and a red hoodie sweatshirt. She picked up her shoes, went out the door into the brisk air and sat on the edge of the deck. The honeysuckle drifted waves of exotic scent her way, enticing her into the morning. Shoes tied, she listened to the silence at her favorite time of day: before the cock crowed, before the chickens scratched, the sun shone, the moon set and the stars faded into the day.

Beth emerged around the thicket of honeysuckle, collecting its lingering scent on her jacket and in her hair. She peeped a quiet, "Good morning" to Fox, who wiggled her fingers, got up from her deck perch and joined her friend on the path.

"Where to?" whispered her new best friend. "Up Saddle Mountain or down Carmel Valley Road to unexplored territory? At least for me."

"Let's cross Carmel Valley Road. I know where we can jump the fence on the other side, up on Los Arboles. If we go up that hill, I can show you my favorite tree."

After they slipped through the fence and waded through waist high, waving green grasses and blue sparks of Lupin and masses of those bright orange California poppies and myriad wildflowers, they came upon a narrow path delicately stamped out before them by the hooves of neighborhood deer. The path led Fox and Beth up along the hill's perimeter, switching back higher and higher until they could see back across Carmel Valley Road and the line of Monterey Pines on Saddle Mountain.

"We're usually sitting up there, talking," said Beth. Fox nodded.

"The oak tree's just a little further."

Now, they sat on a low branch, with another low branch at their backs—a regular oak tree sofa, protected by a canopy of graceful branches and leaves spreading out high and wide.

"I met Fenn Cooper here," Fox said. "I found flowers in little jars and special stones placed just so. 'Dusty' written on a stick in the ground. I was pondering who Dusty was when I heard a voice behind me.

"'It's called Revelation Tree,' said the voice."

Fox remembered the moment well.

"Whoops!" "What?" "Oh!" they said all at once and Fox fell off the branch.

The tall, elegant Fenn Cooper glided (or would it be glid?) into the clearing.

"Sorry. I thought you heard me coming. Fenwood Cooper, namer of trees. Call me, Fenn, with two Ns." He took her hand and pulled her upright.

"Hi. Sorry, did I intrude on your tree?"

Pressed khakis, pale green Hawaiian shirt and two-tone penny loafers gave Fenn Cooper an incongruous put-together look. Did he always hike up the hill through the pucker brush dressed for a bridge game at the country club? There wasn't a bead of sweat on his brow. "It's not my tree," he said.

"But, you've named it," Fox said. "I have a daughter who says if you name it, it must be yours."

"Ah. Well, then, I willingly share it with you. And I'd like to meet your daughter. Who are you, by the way. I recognize your rusty hair."

"Fox Wyman."

"Ah, yes. From Sweet Farm. Glad to know you."

Fenwood Cooper left after a fifteen minute conversation that included tap dancing classes (of which he maneuvered a 10 second example in the dust), his Carmen Miranda Fruit Bowl headpiece for the costume party attended in June (photo in pocket), the estate sale haul for his antique store in downtown Carmel ("You must come visit"), questions about drying lavender for sachets ("Perfect in the shop, right?"), jitterbugging (more examples, this time swirling Fox around the little clearing, more dust involved). And, of course, his mother's wigs, with gesticulations describing the various ways to achieve the proper poofiness of the coiffures with rollers, hairspray, etc. Oh, and Dusty was his dear but late golden lab.

After an invitation to Sunday tea (waving vaguely in the direction of a cluster of old Carmel Stone houses on Los Arboles), he handed Fox his calling card:

Fenwood Cooper, Entrepreneur 408-624-2322

and wandered back the way he came.

"Whew," Fox smiled, as he walked away. "All that and it's not even 7am."

"It's like your own Hobbit House," Beth said now.

"Ha! You're right. I hadn't thought of that."

"It's a good thing, a Hobbit House."

"Yeah?"

"Yes. Everyone needs a place to go."

Fox told Beth her thoughts of the morning. She said, "And it's true, you know. I don't even know what I mean when I say this, but being with you *is* like being alone, only better." Fox was quiet for a minute. There was so much Beth wanted to say, but she knew better than to interrupt.

Fox said, "The thing is, with you? I feel safe. At peace. Like I don't have to guard my back or watch my words. With every single other person on the planet, I am as uncomfortable as if I were wearing someone else's skin on my bones. I love my sisters, but I have never had a friend."

The two women looked at each other with that intensity that comes with the deepest, most connected of friendships— the ones where you know you are family, chosen family, where you hold hands and say, *No matter what, I am there for you. One mile or a thousand, I am there for you.*

Beth's answer was the most complicated of nods: a kind of shrug mixed with a smile blended with a slight tipping of the head and a laugh and a sigh. No words could capture this response, no painting show the feeling.

Finally, Beth asked, "Why Revelation Tree?"

"Fenn says it's because something always seems to be revealed here."

The women looked at each other and laughed.

Chapter Six

August 1964
Carmel

 Tate & Dr. Rose

The doctor's office nestled in the cypress trees in the Carmel Woods area, just north of downtown. Other bungalows made of Carmel Stone surrounded this tiny building, with similar shingles hanging by their doors: Psychiatrist, Psychologist, General Practice.

Dr. Rose Weisberger, psychologist: small, compact and focused. Her wiry grey hair coiled high on her head, making her appear at least 5 feet tall. She wore straight skirts and sensible shoes. Dr. Rose reminded Tate of Sister Helen at the Lucia School—tiny, serious, big brain in small head. She could be anywhere from 40 to 85.

Dr. Rose took an interest in young girls wounded by bullies. Dr. Rose secretly believed most bullies were beaten as children or had small penises. *It sifts down to trauma and the ego,* she thought. The more comfortable one was with oneself, the less force used on others. She became the champion of girls.

In the 1964 small town of Carmel and its surrounding Monterey Peninsula settlements—Carmel Valley, The

Highlands, Big Sur—Dr. Rose knew practically all the girls. If she didn't know them, she knew of them. Dr. Rose made it her professional business to know the population. The boys did not escape her scrutiny, but the girls were her particular milieu.

Behind the closed doors of her treatment room, where we and others may not follow, Dr. Rose sits in a comfortable chair. Her patients sit or lie down or curl up on her couch, usually with a box of tissues. Dr. Rose was the first psychologist in her circle to have stuffed animals and cushy toys in her basket, and Tate lay there once a week, holding onto a rather large purple cow with big brown blinking eyes, long, black, plastic eyelashes and a pink belly.

With respect to the privacy of the therapist's room, we will not enter the sessions. However, Tate said this to Stevie:

"I've been there three times now, Steve, and we talk about everything but That Night. Dr. Rose asked me about Fox, like, what she's like to live with, which took up the whole first hour. The second hour we spent on Deke, and most of the third. He's gonna take up a lot of time, I can tell. You know: what I felt like when he was gone, if I missed him, did I even remember him, did I have a father figure, if so, who was it, how do I feel about boys in general. I think we're building trust—I don't know. It's all right, I guess. At this rate, I'll be ready for my next date by the time I'm 35."

"I'm sorry about that day—with Jolene. I should have told her—I did later."

"I know. It's not your fault at all, Stevie. Honestly, I don't know what gets into me. It's not like they got anywhere, That Night. I fought them like a tiger. And then, Deke. It's just that…they drugged me! They drugged me, Stevie. Boys we know. They actually put that horrible stuff into a bottle of champagne, like it was some kind of joke. 'Ha ha. Let's drug Tate Wyman and pop her cherry for her. Or at least scare the living daylights out of her. Let's change her whole life in an instant.' At my Prom. I will never get over it."

"They told Deke they didn't mean it. They just wanted to freak you out."

"Like that's supposed to make me feel better."

"It was pretty stupid."

"It was more than stupid. It was heartless, and unthinking, and cruel. What jerks."

"They are coming over, you know."

"I know." Tate rolled her eyes.

"With their parents."

"Ugh! I know! Why is Deke making me do this?"

"It's not you he's making do it, it's Todd and Rodney."

"Yes, but I have to be there."

"Well, it's hardly an apology otherwise."

"Will you be there?"

"Oh, cousin, I would love to be in the room for that. I think this thing needs witnesses. Or, really, an audience."

"Great. My humiliation is your entertainment."

"No, see, this is why you need a shrink. It is not your humiliation at all. It is your victory. We will see two idiots get glorious comeuppances from your, you thought, weakling of a father, who turns out to be the hero of the day. We will see justice."

"Justice would put them in reform school."

"Maybe. But, from what I hear from Farley, reform school just makes for hardened adult criminals. This will not help them. Or you. Or the rest of society. But, yeah, if Deke lets me, I'll certainly be there. I wouldn't miss it."

"I'll tell him I need you."

"Tell him you need both your scowling cousins. That ought to spook those little varmints right off the bat."

August 1964
Carmel Beach
The Water's Edge

The selkies called to Stevie, seduced her to the waves. She imagined a pod of feminine-looking seals, with red lips and florescent whiskers, Florence and Mabel and their brood of baby selkies, waiting for her on the rocks. She put the February Good Housekeeping Home Birth Issue aside (She new about home births–she *was* one) and told Dr. Rose's receptionist, "I'll be back in an hour. I am going to hunt for selkies."

While Tate (reluctant interviewee, like her father, Deke), lay on the shrink's sofa with a purple creature in her arms, Stevie walked down Ocean Avenue to Carmel's Main Beach and stashed her shoes behind a rock. She rolled her jeans up to her knees and took off down the dune to the water's edge. The sand felt good between her toes—gritty and sharp.

She walked south along the splashing surf. The afternoon sun was bright. She raised her hand to block the glare, looking for Mabel and Florence and found instead the line of after-noon surfers, sitting on their boards, waiting. Stevie had no desire to surf, the water not her comfort place, but she liked to see the surfers balance on their boards and glide over the cresting waves.

She wondered what surfers thought about, waiting for waves. Girls? Kissing? More dynamic boards? Yesterday's chili cheese dog?

"Majestic, isn't it?" said a soft voice behind her. She jumped a little and turned around. The smallish roundish man grinning at her was about 40, with prematurely gray hair and a salt and peppery mustache. The smile included a lot of very white teeth. Above the smile were the twinkling brown eyes of an ancient gnome. His brown hat sported a dove feather in the band.

"Yes," she blurted. She almost laughed. He was so gnomish.

"You local?" he asked.

"Uhm, yes."

"I'm not dangerous. I'm just new here."

"Uh huh."

"Really." He laughed. "I'm Johnnie Anderson, latest editor of *Monterey Magazine*, at your service." He bowed.

"Oh yes, the mag with a message. How come no one keeps the job there for long?"

"Ah, I suppose the message keeps changing and no one can stay up. Long story, really. Not pretty."

"I can imagine."

"Can you, indeed?"

"Yes. Hi. I'm Stefani Michel. I've lived here all my life." She shook Johnnie Anderson's hand.

"Ah. Wonderful. Perhaps you'll let me ask you some questions." He whipped out his card. "Come to my office, it's in the…"

"Oh, I know where it is. But, I'll have to ask my parents. I'm

15. They'll want to know who this Johnnie Anderson is and why he's interested in their daughter."

"Fair enough."

"What shall I tell them?"

Johnnie Anderson looked her up and down, from her braid to her bare toes.

"Tell them, you look like someone who knows a thing or two about Carmel, California."

"I submitted a story to *Monterey Magazine* once," blurted Stevie, awakening to this opportunity.

"You're a writer?"

Stevie hemmed. She hawed. She thought it over for an instant. "Yes," she said. "I am a writer."

"Well, even better. Come any time between 1 and 3pm. 1-3 is teatime. I'm there slogging away pretending I know what I'm doing."

"OK," she said.

"And bring something you wrote." He turned away and snapped a picture of a surfer leaping from his board as it skimmed across the surf to the sand.

What? Stevie asked herself. *Did I just meet a job-offering gnome?*

Stevie retrieved her shoes. She brushed off her feet and slipped on her sneakers.

Stevie looked back to the surf before turning to trudge up the hill to Dr. Rose's office. Johnnie Anderson was gone.

A few days later, Stevie and her mother, Rita, turned up at the *Monterey Magazine* office in Carmel and stayed from 1 til 3. Tate was involved, too, since she had a driver's license. (Fox, of course, wanted nothing to do with the press.)

Rita liked the thought of tea and brought along a cinnamon streusel coffee cake. She particularly loved that the selkies sent him to Stevie on Carmel Beach. Right up her mystical alley.

If Johnnie Anderson was amazed by this instant party, he did not show it. To his credit, the kettle atop his electric hot plate was large, bubbling and ready to pour. If Johnnie Anderson took life lightly, he took his tea seriously: often, black, no sugar. Rita liked this, too.

Enchanted by Rita's lyrical voice, Johnnie asked her questions to keep her talking. She babbled about farming, and the Tea Room, Maria's quilts, lavender. Stevie and Tate were amused by this, but Stevie soon stepped in to seal her fate.

"Here's my essay, Mr. Anderson. It is 700 words about humming. And here is one volume of my Honors English Journal, which no one ever sees," causing Johnnie Anderson to look up from the page she'd opened for his perusal: a colored pencil sketch of the Hobbit House with a sign that said, "No Boys Allowed."

Johnnie Anderson had struck gold.

June 1964

Humming in Spanish
An Essay
Stefani Michel

Humming runs in our family. Every time I turn around, someone is humming.

It may have started with Mama Maria, well known for singing to her lavender seeds in French and praying over her plants. My grandfather, Poppy, whispered in my ear one day, "Can't you hear your grandmother? She's humming to her lavender sprouts...in Spanish!"

And I did hear it. In fact, I've been hearing it for years without even tuning it in. But I understood Poppy. It's definitely Spanish humming. Hard to explain, but it has a beat, and castanets are involved.

Poppy made me think of all the times I've heard members of my family humming their unique sounds, under their breath...a personal crooning.

When my Uncle Deke was gone, Aunt Fox hummed, "I'm So Lonesome I Could Cry." She didn't think we could hear her. But when she hums, her red hair frizzles. It makes a person turn her way. And if we looked hard enough, we could hear the humming. It was soft, and sad, a lonely heart humming, full of tears she couldn't cry. A moan of humming.

Fáno, on the other hand, hums while he works. His hums are pure Gypsy. Fáno's hums are almost holy, and happy.

My father is rarely upset, so when he hums, it's good to rub up against him, like Mesmer, the cat. It rubs off. His humming is contagious. In a good way.

Fáno attracts Hummingbirds. It's a riot to see him in the lavender fields ducking the bombardment of birds humming around him. He smells like flowers. And he wears red a lot. He just laughs and waves the hummers away. He says the hummers drop "Celestial Raindrops" on his head.

Deke Harley dreams about humming. When he was absent-mindedly wandering around the countryside, he dreamed of Fox, only she was just a girl in red, humming nonsensical, staccato tunes, "like fairies tripping over branches," Deke said.

And Uncle Chuck! Chuck's the most vocal of all. Chuck died four years ago, but the essence of Chuck follows Aunt Nana and my cousin Jolene around, constantly humming. Even Jolene's Grand Mamá Charlotte, Chuck's own mother, reported Chuck's whispers in her ear, from the grave. She described them as "Ta Das!" and "Oom Pa Pas," and he generally waves his conductor's baton around the room. She can hear that, too. She said, "He smells like a Christmas Tree." Jolene said, "No, Grand Mamá, he smells like gin!"

Jolene was spooked by her father's humming from across the Veil, until she performed a ritual at the beach to help put him to rest. She released an imaginary box, full of the guilt and emotions about his death, to the sea. She said at the time, "I don't necessarily want the humming to stop, but I wouldn't mind a new tune."

The consensus on Chuck is that he won't rest until he has had his say. He lurks around, just out of sight, and he'll keep humming until Jolene and her mother sort through all that family dirty laundry. Nana says, "It's a throb in my head, his constant hum. It gives me a headache."

My cousin, Tate, of course, hums in her sleep. She hums while eating, while doing homework, picking tomatoes, riding home from school on the bus. Tate has been humming since she flew from her mother's womb. She says she hums because she doesn't want people to hear her practice, but her humming is as beautiful as her singing. Tate's humming is lyrical, a trilling songbird's hum.

I don't think of myself as much of a hummer, but Cousin Tate says I hum Handel's Hallelujah Chorus when I'm concentrating. But she also says I stick out my tongue about a 16th of an inch and I put my index finger on the tip of my nose, like the answers to all questions lie within.

No matter the language, no matter the tune, humming is a kind of outlet: a release of energy spilled over, an homage to the gods, a love note in the ear of a friend. Humming adds dimension to your emotions. It also seems to be a way for the late to communicate with the living. Amen to that.

# Stevie to Farley

Dear Farley,

I don't have to wait tables at the Warehouse Pizza Parlor anymore. I have landed a job with Monterey Magazine, writing a 300 word column about 1960s life on the Peninsula, from a teenager's point of view. $25 per month. A fortune.

I worried that Johnnie Anderson, the new Editor, hired me as a lark, or a joke, or because he was some kind of lech (we met on the beach). I also, please don't laugh, I also think the selkies, who called me to the beach that day, sent him in my direction. Is that magical thinking? Rita met him and she thinks he's the real deal, and if she approves, then he's OK.

It's not as easy as I thought, coming up with 300 words good enough to be printed for all the world to see. And, the Peninsula is a big place—I have to stretch my mind farther afield than Sweet Farm and Santa Lucia School and Carmel beaches and fables.

Johnnie Anderson says to start at the beginning and kind of introduce myself. So here it is:

On the Bus
Me, Stefanie Michel

For my first (almost) sixteen years of life, my world has been the Monterey Peninsula. I have eaten lettuce and broccoli and strawberries and corn and artichokes and Brussels sprouts from the Salinas Valley, poured milk from the dairy right down the road into frosty glasses right out of the freezer. I am enrolled at a respected institution where I learn to communicate in, generally, the English language (I'll tell you now, I suck at languages, except English, and I'm a complete failure at music, which is just another language, only all mathy, except I can harmonize a little). We do math and sciences and art appreciation and other college prep courses.

I live near the beach, have favorite benches, secret beach coves, very particular flat, sandy spots. No, I won't tell you. I have ridden the bus all over the Peninsula and know the bus routes by heart. I meet people.

I suppose I am as qualified as any local teenager to write about Teens on the Peninsula. Through interviews, conversations and observations "On the Bus," I'll write our stories.

S.A.M.

Tate and Stevie Discuss Teenagers' Dilemmas

"Please don't write about That Night, Steve. You won't, will you?"

Tate worried about her cousin's prolific pen. She imagined the headline: "Carmel Valley Teen Girl Fends Off Drugged Teen Boys in Late Night Kerfuffle," or "Dad Saves the Day and Her Virginity." She'd never find the band now. Boys were the enemy. Boys were deceitful. Boys were just plain bad.

OK, it wasn't exactly in *Life Magazine* or anything. But, that was the point. Tate did not want her cousin writing about it.

"I won't," said Stevie, "but you've got to admit it is a teenaged issue that lends itself to discussion. It has all the components: Girls, Boys, Prom, Drugs, Alcohol, Sex. All the things we deal with every day."

"Yes, but it's me this time, and I don't want to be your story."

"Of course not. I would never write about you like that. I'll think of some other way to write about the modern problems we face that *Anne of Green Gables* never had on her mind, sequestered up there on Prince Edward Island."

"Hmmmmm," said Tate. She thought of something Dr. Rose said the other day. "When I was your age, Tate, my parents and I were escaping genocide in Germany. We hid in basements and alleys, had tussles with the SS, learned how to use weapons for self protection. We lost our families and friends to a madman, we dragged the skeletal barely-living out of their cages at Auschwitz on the day of liberation. We didn't have your problems, but we had plenty.

"And I learned one thing, which is why I do what I do. You cannot shove problems, or memories of problems, under the bed. They will come back to haunt you, grab at your feet forever. Face them head on. Own them. Learn from them. But do not be afraid of them. That is the only way."

Tate was trying, but it was hard.

Midnight wasn't the same anymore. The creative juiciness was gone. She shook herself awake from bad dreams and lay in her bed afraid. She even had difficulty with music, which usually calmed her fretful spirit. Her life was all topsy turvy, and all because of two stupid boys.

If a story is not about the hearer, he will not listen.
And here I make a rule—a great and interesting story
is about everyone or it will not last.
– John Steinbeck

Stevie Makes Her Way

"**M**r. Anderson, I…"

"Come now, Stevie, call me Johnnie," he said, "everyone does, from the milkman to the President of the United States."

"You know the President of the United States?"

"No," Johnnie laughed. "But if I did, he'd surely call me Johnnie. Everyone does."

Johnnie Anderson's gnomishness made him look like a child with fake mustache dressed up in his father's clothes. His face was round and red and cheeky with deep dimples like parentheses around his grin, and twinkles in his eyes, as if he were always amused. His mustache twitched. The rumpled tweed jacket fit loosely over a natty sweater vest. The customary red bow tie was askew. All of Johnnie's pockets seemed to contain something—receipts, cough drops, sticks of gum, paper clips.

When Johnnie (seldom) removed his hat, he exposed an almost completely bald pate ruffled by greying curls. For the first time, Stevie noticed the bristly dark hairs sticking out of Johnnie's ears.

She silently agreed, if the President ever met John Anderson, he would surely call him Johnnie.

"Johnnie, I want to know what to write about."

"You are writing about teen life."

"Yes, but what about it? Should I write about football heroes and straight A students? The Prom Queen? The best burgers and fries in town? You know—the Chamber of Commerce view. Or, should I, could I write about real things?"

Johnnie thought this over. He got in trouble with bosses once by letting someone loose on reality in a fashion magazine. Although, *Monterey Magazine* was different, he still had bosses.

"For instance?"

"I met this girl on the bus the other day. She was about 17 and pregnant out to here." Stevie gestured two feet in front of herself. "We had a conversation. And, also, I was talking to this reporter from the paper and it got me thinking."

"Which paper?" Johnnie asked.

"Well, the Acorn, if you must know. Anyway, she said that, like when she interviewed Deke, well, she wasn't allowed to really write about it. You know, like, ask deep questions or try to solve the mystery or make anything better. She thought the piece could have been so much more—powerful."

"Deke Harley?" A light bulb flickered in Johnnie's head.

"Yes."

"What or who is Deke Harley to you?"

"Ah—my uncle."

Johnnie Anderson sighed. "Oh my. Of course. Sweet Farm. OK, go on."

"Well, OK. I was talking to Virginia Smith—she interviewed Deke a few months ago-"

"Yes, I read it. I know the story."

"OK, so, when she came back to Sweet Farm to see Deke with the draft of the interview, I was there and Deke wasn't, so we talked. She told me her editor made her *tone it down*—those were her words, *tone it down*, because he said the paper should be printing small town news, nothing provocative. So, she wasn't allowed to probe."

Johnnie smiled. "Go on."

"Well, I'm glad for Deke's sake, and Tate's and Fox's, that Virginia didn't write about their personal lives too much, but, it seems to me I have an opportunity here. No one writes about a teenager's real issues. It's not all about choosing Coca Cola or Dr. Pepper or white bobby sox and jitterbugging contests."

Welcome

Every now and then, a breath of fresh air comes through my office door. Welcome to Stefani Michel's column, *On the Bus,* a look at Peninsula Teen Life today, as seen through the eyes of a Carmel Valley teenager.

Stefani's view is not always rosy, but you will agree that it is well-voiced.

 - Johnnie Anderson

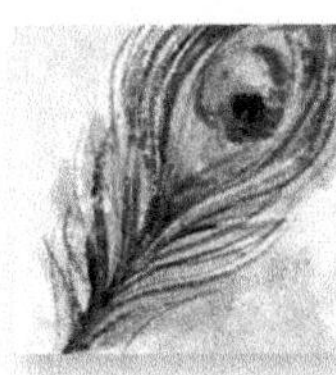

On the Bus #1
Pregnant Out to Here
Stefani Michel

A young girl from San Francisco sat next to me on the bus today. I didn't get her name, but she said she lives "on the street near Golden Gate Park."

When I asked, "Which street?" she replied, "Any street. Safe streets." She literally meant on the street.

There's a shelter nearby where she can get food but she feels safer outside, she says.

A slightly built girl with fly-away fair hair and light red freckles, she looked a little boney under her clothes.

She held her protruding tummy and we both looked down. "I have a baby in here," she said.

"Where will you have it?" I asked.

"I don't know yet. It's early."

"Early? You look nine months pregnant!"

"Almost," she said.

"Where's the father?" asked the 5'2" nosy writer.

"Don't know," replied the girl.

"Where are your parents?"

"They threw me out when they knew."

"What? They what?"

"Well, first they locked me in my room so I wouldn't run away with my boyfriend, Tommy. They were trying to figure out just what to do with me. They wanted me to go to Switzerland for an abortion. When I refused that, they told me I had to give "IT" up for adoption. It's a long story." She rolled her eyes.

"I guess," I said. Lamely.

"Well, when I refused that, they threw me in the street with a suitcase and some cash and I took a bus from the mid west to San Francisco, where I was supposed to meet Tommy at Golden Gate Park. But, that was months ago. He hasn't turned up yet."

"Why are you here on the Peninsula?" I asked.

"Oh, I came down with some friends. I went to Cannery Row to walk around and maybe score and now we'll meet up and go back to the city."

"Score?"

186

"You know, get some weed."

"Don't you have any plan?"

"Plan?" she asked. "Plan for what?"

"Well, for this baby, for one."

"Oh, no plan. We'll go with the flow." She patted her passenger.

"What's that mean?" I asked.

"Oh, you are a country girl. Go with the flow. Let it ride. Live in the moment. If it feels good, do it!"

What was she talking about? She got off the bus at Soledad Street and I'll never know the end of her story.

I have a friend who has a bohemian sister in Big Sur and I imagine she'll know what "Go with the flow" means. Sounds to me like "go wherever the wind blows you." Kinda spineless, but I'll wait for the definition. It's not in the Encyclopaedia Brittanica.

Also, I may be a country girl (and proud of it, by the way) but whose parents lock up their children and then let them go? She can't be much older than I am, and she has a name she didn't tell me and she's alone and pregnant out to here. If this essay were a movie, you'd see me shaking my almost 16 year old head.

S.A.M

The Apology

Deke and Fox allowed the other cousins to be present at the "Apology" on one condition.

Deke said, "You're not to laugh or poke fun at the boys. Oh, I know they deserve it, but they'll get a bellyful without your contribution, believe me. Your presence will remind them of their vulnerability. It's pretty well spread all over town, what they did, so they walk with their tails between their legs already. Their car privileges have been taken away and they have both been grounded for…a long time. Their parents assure us they are extremely sorry, but we have a ways to go yet. Are you OK with this, Tatie?"

Fox watched Deke with fascination. What a difference in him in just a few months. He still had spells, and when overtired, wobbled a bit. He remained soft spoken and hesitant, especially around Fox, and his words were slow to come out, not plentiful, but usually pithy. She did like that about him. But this!

She let him take full charge. He'd managed Tate's rescue without her; he could handle this.

"Can we just get it over with, De?" Tate said to her dad. "The thought of seeing them again gives me the heebies."

They all sat around the big table in the Middle, the family meeting area in the Adobe House, like they were planning a party.

"Of course it does. Sadie will be here, and her parents."

"Ugh! Too many people!"

"Think of it as a kangaroo court. You don't have to say anything, but if you decide you want to, you can."

"I won't."

"You might."

"OK," Tate finally said.

* * * *

The meeting was called at 4pm that afternoon in the Middle. There were no refreshments. Deke and Fáno got right to the point. They sat the boys and their parents on one side of the big table and the two girls, their parents and the other cousins on the other side. Stevie and Jo flanked Sadie and Tate, human bookends, pressing close, shoulder to shoulder.

The boys' side was dwarfed by an overwhelming number of supporters on the girls' side of the table.

Todd and Rodney studied the floor as if preparing for a test on Mexican terra cotta tiles. Their parents looked at the tiles too; they knew what was coming.

When all were assembled, Deke asked Fáno to go outside and greet the surprise guest, Pat Lovell, Carmel Valley sheriff, Deke's new friend and, now, the special protector of Sweet Farm girls. Deke introduced Sheriff Lovell like this:

"You all know Sheriff Pat. And he certainly knows all of you. So, don't go all wobbly, boys, you look like you're about to be carted of to the county jail. You're not. Sheriff Pat is here to share a little information with you."

Sheriff Pal Lovell, known around town as the Singing Sheriff, was a big, beautiful and jovial Afro-American (to use the most popular collective of 1964) former football star, with a head of very fluffy dark curls on which he generally wore no cap. Pat was often found singing for his supper in one of the cafes in the Valley. With his arresting tenor voice, he crooned his ballads and belted out *Caro Mio Ben* with great enthusiasm, endearing him to the hearts of the locals as their personal entertainer as well as their protector. They were proud of Pat when he showed up at the Baptist Church and joined the choir; when he appeared at 10pm at Wolf Hill and hopped on stage (in uniform) with The Ridge Boys and floated some wild hillbilly high notes along with their blue grass harmonies. It was also said he could get your dogs to howl at the moon with him and no one doubted it.

At this moment, Sheriff Pat's smile was pasted on, all business. He agreed to this for little Tate. *She's been through enough*, he thought. *I can at least make her feel safer and make these boys danged sorry they got up this morning.*

Todd and Rodney first heard references to decency, common sense and respect. But, Sherriff Lovell thought that might not be enough, so he showed them movies about driving under the influence, pictures of drugged teenagers and other victims of chloral hydrate, all of it ugly, some with fatal consequences. The boys broke down and cried when they saw a young woman permanently damaged by an overdose of chloral hydrate. They wiped their eyes and studied their hands in their laps, the cat by the hearth, the moth on the screen door. They felt like grilled cheese sandwiches imprinted with boot treads, and looked worse.

As planned in the script of the day, after the boys had been thoroughly thrashed, if not in the physical sense, at least with words and visuals, enough to bring them to tears and get inside their hearts, which was the point, Rodney and Todd got up together and walked around to the other side of the table. The four girls turned their chairs around, and the phalanx of parents moved to the side so the boys could… *Good God,* thought Tate…*so the boys could get through! Oh, Geez, what next?*

Todd, instigator of the foiled event and procurer of the drug in question (he knew a guy who knew a guy who knew a vet somewhere in Monterey County who had enough chloral hydrate to take down a herd of horses) was first to bend his knee in front of Tate, offering her the flowers he'd held in his sweaty grasp for the last two hours.

Todd's mother was afraid he would rebel against all this discipline, these rules and admonishments and shows of strength, this education about the dangers out there in the world. She worried that he had gone too far, gone over the edge, out of her purview, but her son surprised her.

"Mom," he said to her that morning. "I am an ass."

Todd had admired Tate Wyman for several years and would never have done any of this to her if it hadn't been for the stupid flask of 150 proof rum in his pocket and the joints and the coke and a dab of gnarly messed up speed and the ego-crushing looks she gave him when she and Sadie were forced to dance together all evening because Rodney and Todd were such drunken, stoned, slobbering idiots. Oh, Todd had plenty of time to think about That Night (no car, grounded for practically ever and all) and he didn't like himself one bit.

With tears in his eyes, Todd said, "Tate, and you, too, Sadie, but mostly Tate, because…well, because we hurt you the most, I am sorrier than you can imagine. I grovel at your feet because I know what we did was really bad. I…" He tried to hand her the flowers. When she just stared him down, he set the flowers on the floor by her chair. "I will be sorry about this for the rest of my life."

Fox thought, *You've got to hand it to the little delinquent. He's pretty believable.*

Rodney felt bad, too, but his heart wasn't in it as deeply as Todd's; it wasn't his idea, and Todd got him drunk and high in the first place, so he kinda blamed the whole thing on Todd, which affected the sincerity of his apology.

Deke said, "You were an active participant in this mess, Rodney, remember, I was there, so don't tell me you weren't. Don't be blaming Todd for this. Unless you don't have the phrase *no thanks* in your vocabulary. No one forced you to get high as a kite on bad stuff. No one forced you to force my daughter." He made Rodney repeat his apology.

The boys and their parents left at 5:30. Quite a dramatic 90 minutes. Tate uttered not a word—just a blink in Todd's direction when he was at her feet. She thought of the purple cow. She didn't even look at Rodney. Sadie gave both boys a little hand signal meaning something akin to, "Ok, I won't sic my Italian brothers Guido and Tony on you now, but you'd better be truly sorry and never show your faces at Santa Lucia School again."

After they left, Tate tossed the flowers in the bin.

Tate's Notebook #1

Dr. Rose says writing down my feelings will help put That Night to rest. This notepad hardly qualifies as a journal, 'cause I'm not sure it'll go that far, but this is a start. I am not a natural writer like Stevie so I think this will be hard, but Dr. Rose says to let my feelings go and write without thinking too much about it. She calls it stream of consciousness, don't worry about sentence structure, so ok. Here goes.

That Night is the worst thing that ever happened to me including losing my dad for thirteen years. It makes me hate all boys which I know is stupid but really, when you think about it, it's crazy, that two boys from my own neighborhood, well practically, they both live in Monterey, close enough, that those two boys, known to us, could do something so incredibly mean.

The ickiest part was when that person, I can't even say or write his name, that T person, the worst part was when he tried to put his hand inside my PJs. The best part was when I bit him on the shoulder, really really hard, and he flipped his hand out of my PJs in a hurry to check to see if I had broken the skin and I hope I did and I remember thinking maybe I could bite him and give him rabies I had so much venom in me right then. Ha ha.

Another icky part (there were many) was the feeling I had when the drug first hit my brain. It hit me fast! It felt like a

194

thousand ants were building a farm between my ears, busy little carpenters creating their town inside my skull. The ants wove around in circles, and then became bees and wouldn't stop buzzing and the ant farm turned into a hive and all the while I had this house of mirrors feeling, all wavy and woozy, and my body was a noodle swimming around in spaghetti sauce.

I don't remember how long I was woozy, they tell me it wasn't even fifteen minutes before my dad and Felix and Fáno burst through the door like superheroes, and I barely remember the minutes before and after I drank the Tangy champagne, but I do remember opening my blurry eyes and seeing the T person multiplied by three and then there were the two of them on me, the two boys, because Sadie slipped out to call Stevie and then they locked the door. Lucky Stevie was home and answered or I don't know what would have happened.

Could we have fought them off? Were they too drunk to know what they were doing? Crapola, they were sober enough to make their little plan, to drive there, to lock the door! What made them do this?

Well, maybe the poisoned speed was behind it. At least Todd told the truth. That's one thing.

Oh! I wrote his name!

I must be stronger than I thought, for a skinny flat chested girl, because even in my drugged state I managed to fight the two idiot boys and keep my pajamas and robe on. Weakling boys. Drunk, high and crazy stupid weakling boys. A fierceness came out in me, like a cat. Thank God for the fingernails on my right hand, filed perfectly to, I wish, scratch their eyes out. I kneed one of them in the groin, I remember that. I hope I did some damage. Self defensive violence was necessary.

They didn't get what they wanted, thanks to their state of drugged-ness themselves and the quick thinking Sadie and my amazing dad and Felix and Fáno. For a guy with "half-a-brain," my dad can move fast when he wants to. He said it was adrenaline. He says he's gotten a lot better just by being at Sweet Farm and I guess it's true cause he saved the danged day, saved my virginity, although I might have seriously hurt those boys in defense of my own honor. I was by no means giving in.

When they locked the door, for a woozy second I thought it was all over, but something happened inside to make me fight like a she-devil, woozy head and all. Oh, I guess that too is a good thing, I know I'd have found a way to get them off me. I was only drugged. They were drugged and stupid. They'd still be stupid tomorrow.

And even though they keep saying they only wanted to scare me, they were out of control. Their drugged minds took over. I know it now.

Sitting on the couch later with Sadie, watching my dad take those boys to the cleaners, well, I've gotta say, that almost made the whole thing worthwhile, to see him come so alive, so big and powerful, for me.

OK, so all in all, even though it was the worst night of my life, and they are stupid boys and I will never forgive them (they can apologize til the cows come home and I won't care, I don't care if their speed had strychnine in it, I don't care if they say zombies made them do it) my family came through and saved me and those idiot boys didn't even get close to popping my cherry as was their drunken desire, ooh that sounds like Stevie, I'll have to tell her. The end.

August 1964
Sweet Farm, Carmel Valley
Tate & the Old Boys

Tate lay sleepless in her bed, listening to a funny sound. The wind? An unusual, eerie tone worked its way into her ears, buried as she was under the covers.

She sat up and listened harder. The sound was music! Coming from somewhere on the Sweet Farm compound.

What? Tate had to investigate. She put on shoes and a long quilted jacket over her pajamas and slid out the door to the deck. The moon was bright overhead and cast spooky but beautiful shadows. She stood very still. She hadn't been out of the house alone at night, even on the compound, since That Night, so she stepped lightly down the deck steps, listening to the whisper of the music. Only music could draw her out of her shell.

It was a harmonica, and something else, she couldn't tell. She tiptoed toward the sound, to the path around the side of the Barn, off to the left, toward Felix and Juana's cottage.

She followed the sound. Did Felix have a radio playing? If so, she wanted to know the channel—something fantastical, like the sound a hobbit or an elf makes on a—*flute? What is that?*

Tate continued on the path to Felix's and walked to the gate. The top half of the Dutch door to the tiny living room was open and there was Felix sitting on a hearth stool playing his harmonica. That was normal. She'd seen and heard Felix on the harmonica loads of times. But Fáno, lying on the floor on his back with his eyes closed, made the most astounding sounds on some kind of pipe, or pipes. Juana and Rita were there, too, humming. Hey, they were humming in Spanish. She felt the beat—a tune she recognized. She ran home in the moonlight and got her guitar.

That's it! Pan flute! Fáno is playing his pan flute. Amazing. It's been in the bottom of a trunk for 16 years!

Tate stood outside the gate for a moment, about to cut and run, nervous—*I can't barge in on Felix's house at 11 at night in my pajamas.*

Oh, who says? They are Fáno and Rita and Felix and Juana! My people!

When she opened the gate and walked into the house, her life changed in an instant. She laughed, because, as ridiculous as it sounds, she knew she'd found the first Boys.

Fox and Beth

Beth says, "Tell me about Tate."

"Ohhh," said Fox.

"I've just had Tate on my mind since you told me about the Apology. It makes me wonder about her—and you—and, motherhood, in general, which I have not and probably will not experience."

"Oh. And why is that?"

Beth said, "Don't deflect the conversation back to me." Fox laughed. "I'll tell you about that another time. It's its own long story. Specifically, I was thinking about the potential of rape being on every mother's mind, and here, this happens in your own little world, within your circle."

"Don't I know it. I think about it all the time. She is much better off with Deke in charge of things."

"Putting him in charge gives him a lot of responsibility. Is he up for that? Are you?"

"You're talking now about my leaving."

"Well, yes. It's all bound up in a rather complicated knot and I'm trying to unravel it."

"I am not giving over my mothering duties to Deke, if that's what you mean. Not that I've been an exemplary mother. She, Tate, thinks I am a cold fish. And, I am not the easiest person to live with. She's ecstatic to have someone to talk to who actually listens."

"Hm. They vibrate at the same frequency." Beth said. Fox laughed and nodded.

"And what would you have done if Deke hadn't been here that night? How do you think it would have turned out?"

"My father and I have hashed that question to bits. It might have been similar, if he, or I, or some other combination of adults from the farm got the call and showed up at the Campanellas.' This was by far the most powerful. I give Deke all the credit for the outcome. And Sadie, of course, for calling.

"As for my relationship with Tate: I will never abandon her. I love her. But let's just say, in some ways, she'd never miss me."

It made Fox both sad and strangely elated to talk to Beth like this. Elated, because she loved having a friend. Sad, because that friend was not, and would never again be, Deke Harley.

About Beth, Who Faces the Music

Beth dreamed in white. Not black and white. Just white. Hospital corridors. Nurses uniforms. Doctor's jackets. Blood. Dirt. Plants. Food. Pantyhose. Patients, even patients of color. All white. And not flesh white, which isn't white. White.

And everything she dreamed about? As you might guess, all dreams took place in hospital rooms, hallways, operating theaters, or in recovery. All dreams were simply reenactments of her life a-jumble, and all dreams were closer to nightmares, having to do with pain, or blood, or illness, and inevitable death.

And her two breakups. Any dreams, all white.

Beth wanted to dream about life, about hope, but her nights were filled with grief and sorrow, all white. The glare of her nightmares was so bright, she closed her dreaming eyes.

And still, they persisted, those glaring dreams, those bright white nightmares jumping her out of the bed.

At Santa Clara, she slept in the nurses' dorm on her 24 hour shifts. There, her white dreams were so white, she wore sunglasses to bed. She tried a sleeping mask. Lavender pillows. A heating pad. Wet tea bags. Ice.

Every night it was the same. She hated going bed. She knew, sooner or later, it would all be white.

There were goblins in her dreams. In 1963, she read *Where the Wild Things Are* to a little girl in the recovery room and from then on, Beth's monsters took on the appearance of

Maurice Sendak drawings, always sinister but oddly benign, like grinning Cheshire Cats with sharp extended claws. They moved around her dreams, rendered in white, like moving drawings. Not smooth cartoons. The drawings moved like robotic pens scratching all over the paper and maneuvering shapes from one monster head to the other.

Beth's dreams were a schizophrenic's dreams, which scared her socks off. She thought perhaps she could get rid of the dreams by working more and sleeping less, but that didn't go well. And that was sad, because she loved the upside of nursing—saving lives, helping people, solving puzzles.

One early morning, in a strange sleepwalk, she ran down the corridor by the nurses' quarters with a fork held in her hand like a weapon and scared the bahooties out of a patient coming around the corner from the communal shower in his airy "hospital gown" and plastic slippers.

By noon that day, Beth had signed out for an extended leave—her first time off in seven years.

"No one is so valuable they should work every day of the week, month and year," her supervisor, Inge Norbert scolded her. Inge didn't even know about the dreams or the crushing breakups.

Beth pulled the posting from the board in the nurses' lounge out of her pocket and placed a call: *Live-in Home Care Nurse needed ASAP, knowledge of lung issues and treatments necessary, Carmel Valley, 408-624-2322.*

48 hours later, Beth was on the train to Salinas. One might ask, "Hey! Wasn't she supposed to be taking time off?"

Well, yes, that was the idea. But, being completely alone, rudderless, nothing to do, nowhere to go, no one to go with, scared Beth more than white dreams.

Beth's little room at Fenn's gave her just enough privacy: she could hear Mrs. Cooper breathing in the night and could read with her light on. She didn't need more than that.

She thought about Fox and the Wymans. She had to laugh. She came to Fenn Cooper's with monastic ideas in mind, while doing her duty as a private nurse. What she found was the friend of a lifetime attached to a giant family.

She put that into her basket of thoughts and tossed it all around like a salad. It should have scared her more than white dreams, but it didn't.

Beth's dreams came less often now, and weren't so white, like the painter of her dreams dashed a bit of burnt sienna into the pot. Almond. Vanilla.

As a meditation, she imagined a friendship with no boundaries and no baggage.

Tate's Notebook #2

I gave Dr. Rose my first notebook pages which started a conversation, finally, about That Night. Dr. Rose said it was pretty good and revealing of my experience and showed her I was ready to talk.

I disagreed, because writing is a lot different than talking, but I let her ask the questions anyway, because, well, here we are, every Thursday afternoon, for the foreseeable future.

The first thing she asked me is if I felt shamed by it, or if I felt guilty or at fault in any way.

Boy Howdy, that was a loaded question. I asked her if I could tell her next time, and she laughed and said, no, let's get to it.

Here is what I remember I said. Not in order, but it's the gist.

Those messed up boys were completely at fault and I don't feel responsible in any way whatsoever. I invited Todd Jerkhead to my Prom in good faith, I even remember telling Stevie that I thought he was safe, since I'm new at the boy/ girl thing and he was a classmate's brother. I was dressed like Alice in Wonderland, for Pete's sake.

I am not shamed, but I am embarrassed that the whole Peninsula knows about this now, I'm surprised there hasn't

204

been a story about it in the *Carmel Acorn Review*. Stevie has promised not to write about it.

But, if I am embarrassed, just think about what Todd AssHat is feeling, and that Rodney Podney, Poopie Pie Person, too.

Well, that just made me feel like a baby, but Dr. Rose said let it all out, so I am.

She says let it out because if I write and talk about it, I don't have to carry it around in a sack anymore, like a bag of rocks.

It was a good metaphor, because I immediately imagined throwing the rocks at the Two Drunken Dirt for Brains Boys. In my imagination, I knocked them both out.

I did feel better, after.

On the Bus #2
Big John
Stefani Michel

I asked Big John, the regular driver of the bus from Monterey to Carmel Valley, why he drove a bus, when I knew he was retired from being a telephone lineman.

"My boy was killed by a drunk bus driver, Stevie. That was 20 years ago. He was 14. My wife will never get over it. Neither of us will ever get over it, but I am driving this bus in his memory, getting people like you safely to your destinations. That drunk bus driver not only killed my son, he also injured other people and put one man in a wheel chair for life."

Big John said he was bored, being retired, and when he thought of what to do with his time, why, he never skipped a beat. I'll drive a safe bus, he thought, and that was that. Nine years later, he's still driving.

"What happened to the drunk bus driver?" I asked.

"He's serving jail time. Hope he's learning to knit. He'll be there a long time."

This made me think of learning to drive, which I am in no hurry to do. I like the safe bus from Monterey to Carmel, every weekday afternoon at 4. First of all, if I take all my books and paraphernalia (purse, jacket, binders) off the seat next to me, people sit there. I meet interesting people.

Secondly, if I keep my stuff piled up in the seat net to me, I can read or think or do nothing and someone drives me practically to my front door.

I asked Big John if it was OK to write about him in Peninsula Teens and he agreed it was a good idea to let parents know there is a safe bus. That there is good in the world.

This makes me think again of the girl who was pregnant out to here. Because I met her on the bus, I guess, but I'm worried about her, out there in the loosy goosy stuff with no money, no home, no boyfriend and parents who care about themselves more than they care about her. And a belly full of baby.

Well, that baby surely has been born by now—in Golden Gate Park under a bush? In the back of a car? How does she care for it? Who is there to help her?

My rambling thoughts mean nothing. I should have asked her name, at least.

S.A.M

Tate's Notebook #3

I've gotten really good at swearing, at least in private. My family's not big on swearing, except "Crapola" and "Blast" and, of course, Fox's usual "Dammit," which I hear twenty times a day.

But I throw swear words at That Night and Those Two Drunken Dirt for Brains Boys like they were rocks. I imagine them, those dummies with arms and legs, in a line-up against a fence. I have a pile of swear words beside me and I am in complete control of the situation. I have permission from the whole world to heave my anger at those boys, so I pick up rock words, one at a time and give it my best heave-ho. I was pretty good at softball before I gave up sports for music, so I wind up my right arm and sling those heavy words until they smash those boys heads in.

Yes, yes, of course I know I can't do that in real life. I am not a murderer, or a firing squad or vicious or mean. But, I must say that after a good session of imaginary bashing, I feel better.

I guess Dr. Rose was right: my body holds onto the pain and the fear, not to mention the amazing anger, even though I say I'm over it. So I keep throwing.

This does not mean I will ever forgive them, or even pretend to be nice to them, but it does mean that I have fewer nightmares and I'm not so afraid to go out of the house.

The Old Boys help with that, too. I never thought I'd be making music with my Uncle Fáno Michel and Felix Rodriguez, but that's what happened. I'm safe with them, they make beautiful music, even if most of it is like humming in Spanish, and we can practice any time we want. I don't believe I said I'd play at The Party, but I guess I have to now.

Stevie asks her Grandfather

"**P**oppy? What was it like when you met Mama Maria?"

"Oh, I would like to hear the answer to thees myself!" said her grandmother, clacking her knitting needles while Jock and Stevie practiced their birthday toasts aloud.

Jock considered his answer. He contemplated his wife of 42 years. He noticed more white appearing at her temples where the curls escaped her best attempt at control. He saw the beautiful creases in her brow, the fine smile lines around her eyes, a little white in her eyebrows.

In 1922, when Maria Pelletier accompanied her friend, Katherine Mason, to Hudson, Ohio for the Case Spring Fling weekend, Jock Wyman was waiting for her at the train station, along with his buddy and fellow teacher, Sam Turner. Jock was the "ride" by default, since he owned a 1922 Packard Twin Six Touring Automobile, one of three cars on campus, and he was in demand as a chauffeur.

Jock Wyman, 38 year-old confirmed bachelor, didn't know there was a woman of his dreams much less that she would be standing on the windy platform holding her big scarlet straw hat on her head with one hand while trying to keep her drop waist flowy *Lucille* frock in place with the other. Her rich dark hair, always untying itself from its ribbons, flew around her face in a flurry.

Maria's red straw hat escaped into the breeze and flew directly into the hands of her new life. Did she see? Not at all. She watched her hat fly away and into the crowd. Katherine said, "Oh! There's Sam Turner! And look! That man he's with has your hat!"

Maria brushed her hair out of her face and looked in the direction of Katherine's pointing finger.

Jock noticed Maria for the first time, looking at him as if she knew him and was about to say hello.

She thought, *He looks so familiar. Who ees that man with my hat?*

He thought, *There is no more beautiful woman alive.*

The earth moved under their feet.

Jock said to Stevie, "I was an awkward fool, darlin.' Katherine was waving to Sam, so we moved in that direction. I didn't realize the hat was Maria's until she put out her hand, as if to say, 'My hat, please, whoever you are.' And I, the most talkative man on campus, was speechless. Sam had to talk for us both. I gave her the hat. I don't remember uttering one word on the ride back to campus, and it took hours before I came to grips with it, but by evening, when we met up with Maria and Katherine at the Spring Fling Cocktail Party, I couldn't wait to ask her to marry me."

"Oh, eet took you weeks to ask me to marry you. Stevie, I scared your Poppy to death. Eet took until at least 10 o'clock that night before he could even speak to me. And he asked me to marry him by telegram! I still have eet, of course. I will show eet to you sometime."

Jock and Maria were wide open with their love, really

welcoming. Remember how they gathered up the wayward Deke and his mother, Rebecca, upon their arrival in 1963? There was no question. In they came to the family. And Jock and Maria were always willing to talk about pretty much anything.

But, Stevie thought, *if I think I'm going to get either one of them to tell me about the act of sex, I must be losing my noodles."*

Tea & Scones

Fenn Cooper called Fox at the Sweet Farm office to say, "Hon, come for tea. I made lemon curd so put some scones in your basket. I know you've got scones. A little bird told me Rita baked this morning."

Fox heard Beth's laugh in the background and smiled. Deke looked up from the drawing board. The schematic of the farm was spread out before him.

"OK, I'll come. What time?"

"Oh, now. Why not?"

Fox laughed again. "Give me a half an hour."

When she hung up the phone, Fox looked at Deke's blond head bent over the table. He'd been there for hours. She couldn't tell if he was concentrating or lost in a maze of misaligned memories.

She said to the air, "I'm going out for a while. See you at dinner." And she was gone.

Deke looked at the empty space she'd left behind. Unusual. Fox was not the spontaneous type.

Fox arrived at Fenn's door 45 minutes later with a basket of warm scones, a box of berries from the garden patch and a bushel of dried lavender.

"A jackpot," cried the ebullient Fenwood Cooper. "Sachet for days! What do I owe you?"

"Tea should do it," said Fox, who was in love with Fenn's home. She loved coming over for tea, lolling on pillows, relaxing in quiet warmth. Everywhere she turned, opulent, intense, but somehow muted colors leapt at her: velvet and tapestry pillows, rich Turkish and Chinese carpets and buckets of fresh flowers in assorted Chinoiserie. Even the tables and the sofa had rugs. Every surface was covered by a rug. She counted 40, from a full sized 12'-15' black and tan Chinese sculpted thing about two inches thick to a blue and burgundy eight inch square on the coffee table. The coasters, which he did not need since every piece of furniture was covered by a rug, were tiny fringed rugs.

The glowing lamps, Turkish perhaps, with deeply colored glass shades over polished brass stands, provided an eerie light, even in daytime. Dark velvet drapes tied back to let dim light through the thick windowpanes. Dark red paint covered three walls, but the kitchen end of the giant room glowed in pale yellow with bright white cupboards and a big window. A thick Persian runner ran the length of the big oak dining table glowing with glossy white paint.

A mini schnauzer-doodle name Foof curled up in a little basket on a hassock, one eye open following Fox around the room as she fondled a surface, texture, glass bauble, book end or knickknack. So different from her monk's room in the Barn. So busy and yet so calm.

Fenn said, "Mother's been in a tizzy over her red wig and

got her blood pressure up. You know. Beth's helping her and will join us in a minute."

Fenn Cooper's shelves overflowed with books and knick-knacks and photos of Fenn with SFB Morse; Fenn with Bing Crosby on the 17th green at Pebble Beach during the "Crosby" golf tournament; Fenn with Marlene Dietrich in front of the Del Monte Hotel.

Beth came up the steps from the grannie apartment. Every time she came up the steps, she felt like she entered a Persian tent, voluptuously lit and warm and homey. Beth had no home at all, just a 10x10 foot room in the back of a walk-up in the city. Her collection of personal items included an unusable but beautiful Kashmiri copper samovar inherited from her mother, six netsuke figures Beth found in little a shop in Kyoto in 1956, and an unbelievably ugly pillow embroidered with garden twine by her bohemian sister, Peggy, currently living under the name of Sunflower Pie Warner in Greenwich Village.

Scones and Lemon Curd and berries filled their tummies. Fenn heated more water. The three kindred spirits around the little rug-covered coffee table settled in for a serious visit.

Their conversation bounced along like a basketball on the San Francisco Warriors' court floor, gliding smoothly between topics: gardening, Rita's scone recipe, the polished banisters you could see your face in at the Druid building in San Francisco, fashion statements in Greenwich Village (bad embroidery, long skirts, beads and bangles) vs. Carmel

Valley (plaid shirts, jeans, boots and hats), owning a business in Carmel, and back to gardening several times. Fox, in a "no time like the present" fashion, got in the truck and zipped back across the road to Sweet Farm to get the fall vegetable seedlings she saw space for in Fenn's garden. When he protested, Beth said, "Let her do it. She's got enough seedlings to grow salad for the valley."

Fenn was actually happy to see Fox go. Not that he didn't like her. He loved her. Enormously. But he wanted a few minutes alone with Beth.

"So, darlin'…does she know?"

A tender silence followed.

Beth took a moment to ponder Fenn's meaning. There was no use pretending. It wasn't like he was asking, "Does Fox know how to toss a salad?"

Beth shook her head. She said, "Am I transparent?"

"Well," said Fenn, opening this fragile door, this shoji screen of love, sticking his toe in, "I could be wrong, but I'd say you're a friend of Dorothy's. Don't be so shocked. It just takes one to know one."

Beth sighed. "Right. Well, I wondered about that, and it's good to know, about you anyway, but she does not know and you are not going to be the one to tell her, because I can see you're all lit up inside and want to be the one. Please, don't."

"Why don't you want her to know? Love is love."

"You and I know that, Fenn, but she's…well, she's been in a bubble. She has loved and lost a man, in a way you and I can't understand. I suppose you'll hear more on that sometime."

"You mean about Deke Harley? We all know about that, sweetheart. Deke Harley's a mythical heartthrob in my community."

"Yes," Beth laughed. "I am sure he is. But, she thinks of me as her new best friend and I'd like to keep it that way because, it is true…and it is understandable…and acceptable. It's nice, being friends. Fox is confused enough without my…sticking my paintbrush in her color box."

"Nicely said, but who says a word from you about your feelings would go astray? She might like it. Just my gut feeling."

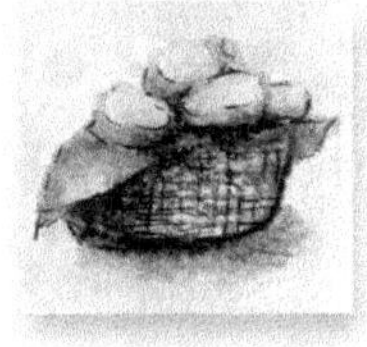

"Leave your gut feeling out of this for now, boss. Here's Fox, back with your seedlings."

"All I'm saying, darlin', is Love is Love."

He took another scone from the basket.

September 30 1964
Carmel Beach, Scenic & 13th
Stevie's Sweet Sixteen

Scenic Drive winds around the jagged Carmel coastline, beaches hugging it like tight jeans on a shapely behind. You drive down the hill on Ocean Avenue, past the downtown shops and cafés, the library, The Normandy Inn, The Green Lantern, The Pine Inn, west and down, slowly down the hill. The coastline vista peaks beneath the cypress trees, sand appears like a slit in the living room blinds, until it opens to the expansive crashing surf and limitless sky.

At Main Beach you can park your car in the big lot, take off your shoes and walk down the sandy hill to the water's edge, to the flat, wet sand, and leave a momentary imprint of your toes.

Turn left, and Scenic Drive meanders south toward the Lagoon, past single walled shacks from the 30s; modern trophy houses with big windows; plein air painters facing the sea; benches and walkways and locals walking their dogs along the path. The trees hang low, Scenic Drive makes way for them. At the Lagoon, with its little bay, the Carmel River finds the ocean and just south, Point Lobos sticks its chin out as if to say, "I am here! Notice my beautiful self."

Drive, or walk, seven blocks on Scenic Drive, south of Ocean Avenue, past the stone houses and clapboard cottages, to a small cove, known locally as "the Bottom of 13th."

Sandstone rocks wrap around the sandy beach, sheltering gatherers. This is the scene of Stevie's 16th birthday party with the family.

After the cars have been parked and the firewood and folding tables and chairs and blankets and picnic paraphernalia have been hauled down the granite steps to the beach, the party may begin. The hole is dug, the fire kindled in the pit, the cooler of cold drinks placed to the side, the coffee and tea in thermoses. Blankets are spread, family collected, hot dogs crackle on the grill, deviled eggs passed around.

Stevie surveys the group from the bench on Scenic Drive, looking down to the beach scene as if she were watching the movie of her own party. No one saw her. Stevie was like that sometimes: slipping invisibly into a room, a class, her own beach party. As an observer, she liked the "fly on the wall" approach.

When Stevie hopped off the bus in Carmel, walked down Ocean Avenue, turned left on Scenic and along those seven winding blocks of Cypress and Monterey Pines, it was the first time all day she thought about her sixteenth birthday, what with tests to pass, a 300 word essay to write for *Monterey Magazine*, library books to return in Carmel, and a deep preoccupation with teenaged existential angst, a concept learned from her grandfather and now pondered daily.

Scenic Drive, the salty air, the pounding of the surf, the squalling and cawing of the seagulls, the scent of decomposing seaweed, all conspire to cleanse from a person the problems, decisions and threats of any day.

Sixteen years old, she thought. *Does that make me a woman? Or did I become a woman when I "commenced my menses," as Mama Maria says? Or am I still a girl? What changes now? Can I make my own decisions, for real?*

Maybe I should first see if I can keep my 8 Resolutions.

If I were Jewish, I would have had a Bat Mitzvah by now. My Mexican friends have Quinceaneras, full-on Coming Out parties, with shimmering glitzy formal dresses. Some girls are presented to Society in white gowns at Cotillions. The Catholic and Episcopal girls have Confirmation.

I am having a beach party. My jeans have a rip in the knee. Oh, and my socks don't match. Welcome to my world.

Soon I'll be away at college. It goes so fast, the time. Two years will flit by in an instant and I'll be off somewhere in the loose stuff, going to college. Like Farley. He's gone already.

Farley. I miss Farley. I hope when I see him again we will be like in the old days. Hm. In the old days, we were kids. No more of that.

* * * *

What are the old days, exactly? To Stevie, at the time of the September Sweet Sixteen Party at the Bottom of 13th, the old days meant everything that occurred before Farley ruined their friendship and changed the entire universe by being an idiot. The old days ignited in spring, 1956, when Stevie and Farley met. She thought of their days hanging out at Sweet Farm, long conversations on the phone late at night, telling each other everything—craziest hopes, loftiest dreams, deepest secrets. That ended on the Ides of March, 1964, the night of his monumental blunder. Seven years. 2,555 days. 61,320 hours. 3,679,200 minutes, 220,752,000 seconds.

Approximately. But who's counting?

At Stevie's Sweet Sixteen
On the Bench

Stevie heard a voice and snapped out of her reverie.

"Hey, Steve."

Stevie thought she imagined Farley's voice, but when she turned around, there he was on the path.

"Well, what in the world…you're here?"

"Happy birthday," Farley said.

"Wow. Thanks. Uhm. Did they know you were coming?" She gestured to the beach scene as she stood up to hug her friend.

"Well, yeah. I know you don't like surprises, but…"

"I don't. But I am glad you're here. I was just thinking about you. Sit down." Rita looked up the cliff and saw the two sitting on the bench. She waved and Stevie and Farley waved back.

"Did you come home just for my birthday?"

"Yes. What were you thinking about?"

"Do you like being away from home?" Stevie asked.

"Ha. That's so you, Stevie. Haven't seen or talked to you in weeks, and you get straight to the point."

"Well, you asked what I was thinking about."

"I did. OK, I'll answer your question. Yes, I like it. I don't like being away from my friends, family, you, but I like being on my own just fine. Mind you, I don't have much free time, but what I do have is mine to fill."

"Do you feel…grown up?" Stevie asked this of the breeze, since she was having difficulty looking at Farley's face. She wouldn't name it…but thing *were* different.

Farley said, "No. I don't feel grown up. Think about it: my father pays my bills, I have a vehicle, a pre-paid Shell Credit Card, food on any of several tables in the vicinity of my pre-paid living quarters, and a job. So, the job doesn't pay, but it's a shoe-in if I want to work for Judge Swann in the future. Life is cake, Stevie. I just have to show up for the Man, you know?"

"The man?"

"The MAN. The boss, whoever that may be at any given time. Right now, the MAN is, collectively, my father, Judge Swann and UC Berkeley. If I have to go into the military, the MAN will be the US Army. I probably won't, because as we both know, I can't see worth crapola. For you, I suppose the MAN is Johnnie Anderson."

"Ha ha, or Santa Lucia School!"

"Yes! Dominican nuns are the MAN!"

"Oh, I've missed you, Farley. I'm glad you came."

"I missed you, too, Steve." Farley, too, spoke to the breeze.

On Turning Sixteen
Stefani Michel

One day you're scrounging in the Toy Box
Looking for the bears and Goldilocks

Playing with crayons and paper dolls
When all of a sudden, your new self calls

You go from reading Nancy Drew
To epics, like Taming of the Shrew

Your body changes, your attitude, too
And no one can tell you what to do

It's something only you can know
Your guides can't tell you where to go

October 1, 1964
Stevie's Little Red Book
The Day After

Farley came to my family beach party. I am glad, but it was awkward. Now that I think about it, when we talked, we looked everywhere but at each other's faces—the sky, the sand, the fire pit, the rocks, the sunset surfers.

Sweet Sixteen. I know too many sixteen year olds who aren't the least bit sweet. Maybe it's just that the double vowels go together. Does anything really change?

My Carmel Valley is changing, I know that. At the mouth of the valley, the Hatton Dairy, that beautiful ranch with white buildings and fences and waving green grasses and lucky cows is going away, and a shopping center called Carmel Rancho is going in. Hard to imagine no dairy, no frosty milk bottles, no ranch, no waving tall grasses and lucky cows. A shopping center!

Yesterday I was fifteen, a girl. From the country. Today, a junior woman. Living practically next door to a shopping center!

I think I'll wear eye makeup to The Trio Party. Never mind.

October 1964
From Farley Simpson
Berkeley

Dear Stevie,

I hope your actual birthday was all that you wanted—just family and a fire at the beach. It was good to see you, even if just for a few hours.

This next month will be light on the work schedule for me since Judge Swann is in Alaska at his hunting lodge, lurking around the woods with a loaded gun in his shaking old hands. He asked me to go with him, wet cigar in his mouth, and grunted like a hillbilly when I said I didn't hunt.

He's a classic. "Boy," he said, shaking his walking stick at me, "any red-blooded American tadpole ought to sit in a wet duck blind with a gun in his hand. Didn't your daddy teach you?" I responded truthfully that my father gave up on me at 12, when I brought along your copy, actually, of Catcher in the Rye *to read while he and his cronies shot at various four-legged creatures they pounded out of the briar patch. To save face, my father told his friends my eyesight was bad and my glasses too thick to line up a shot. That was true, too.*

All above is to say that I'll be back in Salinas for the weekend of The Trio Party, so I'll see you then. I didn't tell you at the beach, but I have picked up

226

the guitar again. It comes back easy as 3.14, chords and melodies written on my skull like scrimshaw on ivory. New songs, too.

You asked me at the beach if I felt grown up and the answer at the time was no, for the reasons I listed. However, I will also say that even though I don't feel particularly grown up, I do feel like a man and not a boy. I am old enough to be drafted, go to war, vote, marry. No, I don't pay my own way, yet, but it's been planned that way, and I have an opportunity to segue into adulthood, to a job, to making a family, raising kids. I'm lucky. Some of my friends in Salinas are working two jobs already: Hank Jones is supporting the very pregnant Amy Shaw through cosmetology school by working in an all night gas station on Highway 101 after humping concrete up a ramp all day at a construction site.

And Hen Pedigo was drafted. This means he'll be going to Vietnam. He says he wants you to hold onto Isabel, the Red Edsel, for him. I told him you don't drive. He said even better. He had a dream he was supposed to leave it with you.

Life is funny, Steve.

Love, Farley Simpson,

Esquire in progress

October 1964
Enter Peter Monk

Peter Monk blew onto the Central Coast with the west wind, after a few years in Hawaii growing cannabis on the Big Island. Peter Monk brought more with him than the nefarious weed. He brought a range of senses that would finally stir Stevie Michel into womanhood, with enough horsepower to drive a truck.

If Aunt Nana's adage was true, that "love is blind and sex makes you stupid," then the sixteen year old Stevie was suddenly prepared to shut her eyes and flunk out of the rest of her plans, if it meant she would find love with this amazing creature.

Peter Monk embodied everything Farley Simpson was not: feral and free-spirited, with chestnut hair down to his waist. His great physical shape came from surfing around the coast line of the Big Island (not to mention hauling rocks and dirt at his cannabis farm), and his hair glistened with mica and smelled of the sea. Peter's face beamed with a genuinely happy smile from being mildly high most of the time and he was ever-ready to play.

Also unlike Farley, sadly, his moral code was a bit askew, since he neglected to tell Stevie about Rhonda Hesselbein, expecting their love child any day now on the Big Island, but that comes later, with its own baggage.

All Stevie Michel knew was that this auburn-haired young god, arbiter of coolness, wanted her. And she wanted him.

They literally bumped into each other in the doorway of *Monterey Magazine*; she, coming in, to give Johnnie Anderson her 300 words for the month of November; he, going out after a brief tête-à-tête with Johnnie, with whom he placed a full page ad and schmoozed a bit about his other business, Monk's Big Island Bamboo. He had plans for the Mainland sales of handmade bamboo furniture from his father, Peter Monk, Senior's "retirement" island estate. Young Peter was setting up shop in Sand City, the tiny Monterey Peninsula town with affordable warehouse space.

For the record, Peter Monk, Junior, entrepreneur, worked alongside his father's furniture-making staff during the week. He spent his weekends on "surfing expeditions" and tending his "crops" on the other side of their island compound, later stuffing it into the legs of his father's creations to "move," as it were, unbeknownst to Peter Monk, Senior, for the last four years. This is, perhaps, just to further show that our Peter Monk, Junior, was a sly fellow.

The 23 year-old already brimmed with New Age ideas before the phrase New Age had even been invented. For a while there he couldn't decide whether to be a minister, a shaman or a businessman. He chose all three, but just called himself a "furniture salesman."

On the plane from Hawaii, Peter Monk contemplated the prospects of his new double life. The mother of his heir on the island didn't really care what he did, as long as he didn't bring it home. By the time he landed at Monterey Airport, he was excited to explore.

So, a few months later, when the collision in the doorway of *Monterey Magazine* brought him face to face with the beautiful, charming and smart but innocent little ¼ gypsy girl, Stefani Awena Michel, just before he was to fly back to Hawaii for the birth of his child, he couldn't believe his good fortune.

Stevie was looking down at her 300 words of the month as she opened the door to Johnnie's office. She caught Peter Monk's scent before she saw him: surf and sky and musk, all rolled into one enticing essence that spoke across the airways and hit Stevie in the solar plexus like Cupid's dart.

First she bumped into his chest, a direct scent hit to her nose, which confused and enthralled her.

"Oh, sorry, sorry," she said to his shirt, then lifted her eyes to his face, and fell in love.

"Well," said Mr. Monk. "And hello to you, too! Who might you be, all serious and studious?" His eyes looked into her like a scope, the sun came out with his smile, she noticed a tiny dimple in his chin.

"Erhm." She cleared her throat. "Stevie. Stevie Michel. Hello."

"I'm Peter Monk, your devoted servant. And I mean it from the bottom of my heart." He gave her the look he offered a woman worth pursuing; a kind of come hither, be mine, I will give you everything gaze that penetrated her already smitten heart.

For once in her life, Stefani Michel was speechless. She took in Peter Monk in a thorough scan, from top to bottom, you know, every inch and every emanating aura. She saw this young, beautiful man in all his loftiest glory: his hair braided with a multicolored ribbon, white shirt and pants, lightweight and rippling in the air current. She noticed his sandaled feet, the leather bag hanging over one shoulder, a sheaf of paperwork in his hands. His thin but muscular body rippled with vitality. He was tan. His blue eyes, the color of the sea, never left hers.

"I…erh…have an appointment…" were all the words in her vocabulary.

"I'll be waiting," he said.

Tate's Notebook #4

This will be my final entry in my notebook about That Night. I think I've written enough and if I keep on, well, it feels like digging a deeper and deeper hole with no bottom. I've already called the idiot boys every name I can think of, I have vented my feelings, I have cried buckets of tears on Dr. Rose's couch, I have spilled enough beans to cover the floor of the Tea Room and I am about tuckered out.

I have decided to leave the anger and put the energy into my music, because I always feel better when I am playing the guitar or making music in some way. I might even go back to the piano, although I remember kicking and screaming on my way to lessons when I was eight. Maybe I won't kick and scream now. Maybe I won't take piano.

I guess the final thing I have to say about That Night is that it took my childhood away. Stevie and I have both been sheltered in the Wyman family, and I don't think we are wise to boys or anything outside of this farm. My mother may be a cold cod of a woman, but she and everyone here—they are like a den of bears. The den takes care of each other and everybody guards the gate. We go to a girls' school. We make paper dolls or knit or create anything we want in the studio with Maria, we eat in the Tea Room, we play or talk or sleep in the Hobbit House. We have five mothers and four fathers here.

It's time we got out in the world. I need to talk to Stevie about this. I don't think she realizes what we have to face "out there." Talk about sheltered. She's more naive than I am—was.

End of Vent.

Chapter Seven

On the Bus #3
Karl (not his real name)
Stefani Michel

Karl takes the bus to school in Monterey because his official address is in Monterey at his mother's but he lives with his father in Salinas. His parents are divorced. So, long bus rides.

I asked him how it was, living with divorced parents. He said, "It's ok. Better than listening to them fight." That made me sad.

Probing, I asked what they fought about.

He said, "Oh, ridiculous things that don't make sense. They really hate each other. They only got married because of me. You want an example of a stupid fight? The best one is, my dad brought Chinese food home when he was supposed to be picking up a pizza, and my mom threw it at the wall. Containers and all. He ducked when she aimed the hoisin sauce at him. It splattered on the mirror in the dining room. She throws things. He yells. She cries. He stomps around.

It's funny, there's like, static in the air when they are in the same room. Believe me, divorce is better in this case. They are both much nicer people when they are not near each other."

I asked him why he chose to live with his father. I was expecting an answer like, "Dad's better at helping me with my math homework" or "My mother drinks" or "Monterey High has a better football team."

He said, "That's where the motorcycle is."

Honors English Journal
Summer Research Project

March on Washington
MLK's I Have a Dream speech
Nobel Prize

Back in the 1940s, A. Philip Randolph was head of a brotherhood called Sleeping Car Porters, sort of a union. He was also an elder statesman of the civil rights movement, going back to 1941 when he protested blacks' exclusion from World War II defense jobs.

Martin Luther King, a Baptist minister and the beloved civil rights leader who is the spokesman for and face of the Civil Rights Movement, was planning a march on Washington for freedom in August, 1963. He joined forces with Randolph, who is still at it and was planning a march for jobs. And the passage of the Civil Rights Act.

President Kennedy met with the two leaders of the March on Washington, as it has come to be called, before the event. He worried the event would "end in violence." He told them he thought the march was "ill-timed."

Dr. King told the president, "Frankly, I have never engaged in any direct action movement which did not seem ill-timed."

The march went on. There were many speakers, actors like Ossie Davis and Ruby Dee. Marian Anderson, Joan Baez, Bob Dylan and Mahalia Jackson all performed.

Dr. King spoke last and his I Have a Dream *speech might become the most important message in the whole civil rights movement.*

I read that Dr. King wrote the speech the night before, it was longer than planned and, in a delivery I won't ever forget, with references to the Bible and the US Constitution, and right out of his big ol' heart, just plain made sense. Dr. King said that America had given the Negro people a bad check, marked "insufficient funds," meaning there was no great freedom or opportunity for them, as promised.

He said, "I have a dream that my four little children will one day live in a nation where they will not be judged by the color of their skin but by the content of their character."

and

"I have a dream that one day the nation will rise up and live out the true meaning of its creed: 'We hold these truths to be self evident; that all men are created equal.'"

It is now October, 1964, and it was just announced that Dr. King is being awarded the Nobel Peace Prize. Progress in the rights of all men.

My grandfather says that race is nothing but degrees of melanin in the skin, and cultures are simply about geographical habits and the weather. Tell that to the white people who think they are superior. Not being all "white" (I believe so-called "gypsy" blood is considered "colored"

*in some circles), I have my own opinions. If my ¼ "gypsy"
blood makes me colored, what does than mean to the other
¾ of me, created from Caucasians from Scotland, Wales
and France. My father is dark, my mother platinum blond,
my Aunt Fox has red hair and freckles and for some reason,
I look like I just stepped out of a Mayan cave.*

*Also, as there have been no race riots, marches or issues of
this nature in my little Mid Valley community, I am not the
person to comment on the color of a person's skin, except to
say, I don't get racism at all.*

Sunday
A New Friend

Stevie introduced Peter Monk to her family as a "friend in the import business," which was true, as far as it goes, if stuffing the hollow legs of Hawaiian furniture with Maui Wowie and Big Island Dreamowski qualified as imports. Stevie was, so far, unaware of this little business detail.

But, the Wymans, Harleys and Michels greeted Peter with equanimity, sizing him up by the polish on his sandals, his clean toes and the luster of his luxuriant hair. Secretly, everyone in the room (Jock, Maria, Fox, Rita, half of Fáno, Deke, Tate and Juana) thought the two of them together—Stefani Michel (small, compact, smokey old soul gray eyes, long black braid) standing next to Peter Monk (tall, lean, beautiful sculpted face, penetrating blue eyes, chestnut braid)—looked like priest and priestess.

Peter Monk did nothing to disabuse the family of *this* idea. He liked it. *What a lovely specimen of female*, he thought of Stevie. The perfect little opposite of the tall, skinny, airheaded blonde ex-model Rhonda. Peter, who fancied himself a bit of a magician, wrapped them in a glowing light, and everyone thought the duo perfect for each other.

Except that other half of Fáno, who took some time, tuned into his daughter and into this Peter Monk, and, in the quiet process that was his way, felt something wobble in the cosmos. His head cocked and his ears twitched, like Misty, the beagle. He didn't know what it was yet, but the sensation was there: a cloud-quake, a shiver, a shudder.

Not all was perfect in Paradise.

Tate was surely wrong about Stevie's innocence because at the very moment Tate was writing #4 in her Notebook, Stevie was at Point Lobos receiving an education. Let's just say that when she emerged from behind their hopefully private rock, and she dusted the sand off her jeans and ran her fingers through her unbraided hair, she was a tiny bit wiser about the joys of nookie.

Oh, Peter Monk is not stupid, remember, so he didn't go too far with this naive 16 year old, but she'll never be the same and she, once again, is getting love and sex all muddled up.

Should she be falling in love with Peter Monk? Or should she keep that horse in the stall and just let this young god awaken her physical body and leave the rest alone?

Is it possible? She wants it to be, but she doesn't think too much of her usual strategy just now. Plus, she isn't sure exactly how to react or proceed with this. Just a few months ago, the family was protecting Tate from rape and here Stevie is, behind a rock with the gorgeous, sensuous bohemian Peter Monk, whom she hardly knows but wants to trust with her virginity.

And, even though Stevie's mind is generally full of cerebral thoughts about any subject, right now she just wants to enjoy her bruised lips and the sensation of butterflies in her nervous system.

That is kissing! Who cares if we hardly ever talk.

What was that resolution about no kissing? Oh, that was when I was fifteen.

Peter Monk drove his shiny new Mercedes to San Francisco for a little confab with his Man in the City. The time away from the Peninsula gave the young entrepreneur an opportunity to imagine his future.

Ah, he thought. *The best of both worlds.*

How long, though? Soon or later, Stevie will want to go to Hawaii, Rhonda will bring the heir home to introduce to her mother in Santa Barbara, far too close for comfort.

Well, we'll cross that bridge when we come to it. Meanwhile, I have a protégé to train in the art of pleasure. How fun. From there, who knows?

As he drove, he sniffed his little habit and dreamed up wild pictures of himself and his two women, superhero and heroines at the least, and by the end of his 2 hour drive to the City, he ruled the world with his little harem at his side.

Stevie had no idea what was in store for her with this beautiful, shiny slime ball. We, of course, do, and we can now begin to worry.

Fox leads the Way

On the Wednesday before The Party, Fox rounded up the entire farm family at 10am, like Bo Peep gathering wayward sheep with a giant hook. The hook was breakfast. The smell of bacon. The promise of strawberries and pancakes. Fresh cream provided by Elsie the cow across the road. All spread out on the Tea Room counter.

Up! Up! She got the sleepy ones out of bed and the busy ones in from the field. Fox's organizational skills, honed by years of keeping farm and family together, were tested by the explosion of creativity surrounding The Trio Party.

Fox said, "I don't know how this got to be more like a reunion or a wedding than a simple birthday party, but by the time we were finished incorporating everyone's ideas and surprises and songs and specialty menu item into the plan, it turned out this way."

Fox spread the schematic of the farm out on the counter and, with a bamboo skewer pointed out five food stations, two bars, and the stage to be erected over the next two days by Fáno, Felix and Deke Harley. The dance floor, coming Friday with the tents, tables and chairs, would roll out at the appropriate moment.

"The caterers arrive at noon on Saturday, the guests at 5. Meanwhile," she explained, "there is a roving band of relatives and friends from out of town so the Tea Room is set up as the Hub, with a continual flow of coffee, tea and snacks beginning Thursday morning at 10." Fox produced a list of everyone's "Turn at the Urn"—one hour shifts behind the counter and in the Sweet Tea Room kitchen to make it all work out. "There is also a list of who is staying at what inn or guest room and who is expected at the various mini parties throughout the weekend.

"For instance," said Fox, "On Friday night, we have dinner at Graciella's in the Village with about 20 nearest and dearest, for which we've taken over the front room—here is that list. The star means they need a ride from wherever they are staying. The menu is already chosen, family style.

"And Saturday afternoon at 2 is the High Tea in Lavandula for Jock and Maria's Lavandula & Steinbeck cronies. Rita and Juana are doing the tea, and when they are finished, they will turn over the Tea Room kitchen and facility to Jack & Jill Catering for the barbecue. We've set up some outdoor prep area for them, but they'll need the sink, the water and the oven for a while.

"We've ordered two 10 x 10 tents, one for the babysitters and children, with art projects and cushions, and one with a few comfy chairs near the dance floor and stage. The food will occur in several stages: the salad bars first, then the grilling areas with the protein and breads, a station for side dishes and whatnot and then the dessert and cake stations over in the shade by the dance floor.

"We have three of Tate's young music pals who call themselves '2 Guitars and an Autoharp' to open the show for Tate at 6:30. Then Tate and the Old Boys at 7 for about 45 minutes. The Ridge Boys will play for an hour or so of dancing after that."

Fox looked over at Tate, who blushed down to her elbows. Fox cocked her head and raised her brow to say, "Shall I go on?" Tate nodded.

"So, as you know, this is the debut of 'Tate & the Old Boys.' She's asked to be sandwiched between, as she says, 'something corny and something really good, so we don't look so bad.'" Fox looked at her daughter and said, "Honey, we all know you'll be 100% fabulous."

And to everyone else, she said, "The point is, no matter where you all are at 7, get yourselves to the stage."

On the Road
With Lady Charlotte

Lady Charlotte Huffington settled herself into the gray leather seat of the DC8, arranging her little blue pillow just so and barely covering her long legs with the tiny blue blanket.

The seat next to her remained empty as passengers streamed through Charlotte's section of the plane to find their seats in Deluxe. *Good*, she thought. *Perhaps I'll have no seat mate this trip.* She remembered her last flight to New York on her way to California four years ago after Chuck died. That nouveau riche American lady, Formosa De Longue, that was her name, shrill voiced and dripping with arctic fur, harangued Charlotte for 11 hours straight.

On this flight, the Lady was so far blissfully alone.

Will Cameron was last to board the DC8 leaving London Thursday, October 21, 1964. He was breathless and loosened his tie. Brown curls escaped their careful combing and spilled into his eyes.

He rolled those eyes when he saw his seat mate for the long flight to the States. *Why do I always get the old harridans? Shall I hear about tea? Hiring good help? Oh, God, her water color painting class! Or, "Ohhh, I saw you in* The Elixir of Love!!!!!"

He stuffed his carry-on bag into the overhead bin, took off his jacket and was about to fold it when the First Class stewardess took the jacket and hung it in the little closet by her station. He sat down, looked out the tiny window and took in the lady beside him: substantial bosom, long legs and fluffy white hair.

The Lady in question watched the man make his way to his seat. He looked familiar. Did she know him? Maybe he lived in her neighborhood? She looked out the window so as not to make eye contact. He might look familiar, but she did not know him from *Adam*. Blast. No longer blissfully alone.

Flight 4568 was on it way. The stewardess, long, lean, blonde and physically perfect in a British Airways blue suit, stockings and high heels, tottered 'round with small glasses of champagne for the First Class passengers. The girl's jaunty little navy blue hat—a cross between an Army lieutenant's cap and a beanie—was pinned to her perfect hair.

Cory, veteran stewardess of First Class flights on British Airways, knew all her passengers' names. This was before "coach service" was invented, when all flights were either First Class or Deluxe. Before in-flight movies. (Who had time for movies? It was a party! Champagne, hors doeuvres, dinner, dessert, wine and lively conversation. In 1964, the airlines still competed with ocean liners for transoceanic travel, so they put on the Ritz!)

Cory offered the champagne first to Lady Huffington, who took the glass and said, "Thank you."

I hope these two talk, Cory thought. The small First Class cabin was deadly boring if passengers didn't hit it off. She said, "You're welcome, Lady Huffington," as she offered Will the other glass.

Cory the stewardess knew Will Cameron was a big shot opera singer, and there was the telltale penciled-in star next to his name on the passenger list, so she was careful not to mention it.

But Will heard the "Lady Huffington" and looked at his traveling companion. Well. This was interesting, after all.

After Cory delivered shrimp cocktail and tiny crackers spread with sweet cream butter, Will took the plunge. He wanted to be careful. He was mightily afraid of offending the Lady.

Will was aware that if one took away his beautiful voice and star status he was just the son of a well educated middle class bohemian painter. Beva Green Cameron Slade's bigger claims to fame were her marriages. First to a Scottish merchant, William Cameron, known in the family as The Father, so you can imagine all the love flowing around him. After fifteen years of carefree widowhood, she tied herself down to a Cornish horse breeder named Stewart Slade, to whom she referred simply as Slade.

A side note and perhaps the most interesting detail about Stewart Slade was his death in 1958 when his prize mare, Panama Mary, rolled over on his face while suddenly expelling twin colts in the night during Slade's birth watch. Beva nicknamed the colts Stewart and Slade in his honor.

Will had no blue blood to offer Nana, and therefore, Jo Huff. He was simply a middle aged tenor in love for the last five years with an unavailable American woman, now a widow. If he had any baggage, it would be himself. His mother could outwit Winston Churchill in the polite discourse department.

He turned to his companion and said in his mellifluous voice, "Lady Huffington, may I intrude? I believe we have mutual friends." *Oh, son of a biscuit. Mutual friends, Will?*

The Lady gazed at him over her imaginary lorgnette. She took off the actual half glasses and looked at the man.

"Indeed?" she said, arching one eyebrow. *Hm. Where have I seen that face before? Heard that voice?*

Lady Charlotte bailed on her puddle jumper flight to Monterey from San Francisco and accepted Will's offer to drive her down to the Monterey Peninsula in his Hertz rental car. How could she resist three hours in a red Chevrolet Impala convertible seeing the California coast with a handsome tenor? She hoped someone thought he was her gigolo, squiring her around the country. Besides, she didn't like puddle jumpers.

What a fine time they'd had, flying across the Atlantic ocean and then across the USA, two posh Brits on the way to a very American family party. Their American family.

Charlotte took to Will immediately. She was hungry for experience, bored to tears by her life, and excited to be going to America to be with the Sweet Farm girls. She no longer thought of them as hicks and heathens.

Now, this unexpected boon—she'd already decided to think of Will as her sort-of-son-in-law.

She thought no one should call her Lady Charlotte during her week at Sweet Farm. Nor even Mrs. Huffington. Charlotte would do. Or Grand Mamá Charlotte.

"How about Charlie?" asked her new friend, Will. She gave him a look.

It was hard to tell who was whose captive audience on that plane ride. Will told Charlotte stories of his career, of back-stage at the Met, of a girl he left behind because she couldn't sing an F above high C as Mozart's Queen of the Night. That wasn't the reason he left her—but her emotional outburst over it was the last straw.

Charlotte told Will about her husband's errant behavior, her sons' strange choices, her mother's penchant for a frozen mango lassi with a shot of vodka for breakfast.

Will talked of his mother's paintings, his late sister, his absent and then late father, the stepfather, Slade and his string of mistresses, about which his mother still knew nothing. Charlotte thought, *Hghmph. I'll bet she does.*

When Charlotte talked about her son, Charles, Will started to cry. She told the story backwards, like Chuck was Dorian Gray. She said, "I hardly remember anymore what Charles was like as an adult, but I remember his little tow head and his soft white shoes and chubby little legs. I remember his first words, 'Ba, bebe'—'bottle for the baby,' but not his last words. I remember the night he was born but don't quite remember how he died."

Will blurted out, "I have loved Nana for years, Charlotte."

Charlotte said, "I know."

The windblown pair arrived at Sweet Farm just in time for the family dinner at Graciella's in the Village. Nana squeezed into the front seat between Will and Charlotte, the three cousins piled in the back and tied scarves around their abundant hair. Deke and Fox followed in the Sweet Farm truck with Becca Harley, who arrived that afternoon by her preferred mode of travel, the westbound train. Jock drove the Cadillac with Maria in the front seat and Rita and Fáno in the back.

Nana was surprised by Will and Charlotte. She'd been worried when she heard they connected on the plane and were driving down together, and here they were, getting along like—like friends, laughing, like they'd known each other forever and had secrets. She was both pleased and perplexed. How was this then, that her husband was dead but hovering and her lover was buddies with her mother-in-law?

The three vehicles arrived at Graciella's about the same time, where Farley met them at the door. Everyone was pleased to see Farley, including Stevie, though she didn't know what to say about her boyfriend.

Was he her boyfriend? Peter Monk had moved smoothly into her life. He was chivalry itself, but in an insistent way, as if she were his to squire.

He had walked her to the bus stop the day they met, waiting until she was seated before he turned to go. Since then, he met her at the beach twice and for tea at the Bakery in downtown Carmel, where they ate flaking croissants and stared at each other over untouched cups of Earl Grey. And then, Point Lobos. They hardly talked. She knew very little about him except that he imported his father's furniture from Hawaii.

She had pulled herself together after the festival of kissing behind the rock. She'd go from reveling in its glory to shame and embarrassment, although no one knew, and then to shaking her head, like a wet dog, to get Peter Monk and his lips out of her head.

She wasn't sure she could share any of this kissing story with Tate. It's one thing to blab about an aborted kiss, but this. This just seemed…fraught. And private.

Meanwhile, there was Farley. In Stevie's mind and general consciousness, her best friend, next to Tate and Jo, of course. She "best friend" needed him now, didn't she? Crapola. It's suddenly gotten complicated again. Just when she wanted to talk to Farley the most, *that* kiss was still dangling on a string in front of her face. There was no way she was going to be able to talk to Farley about kissing someone else.

Tate? No. She was caught up in her rant against all boys/men, so, no.

Jo? No, she didn't think Jo *or* Tate would understand, considering Tate's recent experience and Jo's lack of experience. Nope. This was just one more secret to keep.

In Farley's mind? Who knew? It's not like she hadn't made it clear. So, she'd just let the chips fall.

Farley, meanwhile, enjoyed himself immensely at Graciella's, sitting between Stevie and Tate, his best pals. Thank God Stevie was mostly back in his life. And across from him was the fascinating Will Cameron, who had a practiced grip on the conversation—tuned to every utterance, with a quip for each. He was dashing, which was curious, because he was warm and soft, not fat, but comfortable, and easy, like Farley. *But socially,* Farley thought, the *man's adept!!* He slowed down to like 33⅓ to talk with Deke, sped up to stay with Fox's mind and took Becca's hand in his when she told him her story. Farley studied Will Cameron.

Farley also whispered and plotted with Tate about her debut and Farley's, too, since he intended to sing in public for the first time at The Party. It brought him and Tate together in a new way, deepened their friendship, united them before the prospective audience.

Stevie was oblivious, for perhaps the first time in her life. Her mind was wrapped up in her new romance, her vision clouded by memories—already she missed Peter's surf scent, his self assurance, his plans for the future, and of course, the warmth and the taste of his lips.

How dull her life seemed, without him. He completed her. He made sense. Everything else was trivial. He must be her boyfriend. Time for her to forget this separation of love and sex business and just let herself love the man. What did she have to lose?

Chapter Eight

The Party

It was a three-butt stage, Deke said, and at six inches off the ground, plenty high enough to see over the crowd and have the crowd see you. Its backdrop was the wide back wall of the Barn, the rented stage lights gave it a soft red glow.

Fox was on the stage now taking firm but shy command of this gathering. She welcomed all the guests, mentioned who had traveled the farthest (Grand Mamá Charlotte beat Will by three and a half miles), and who was the youngest (Betsy's granddaughter, Eva, three months). After a few housekeeping tips (honey buckets in the parking lot, sand pales for cigarettes, wander in the fields until dark, watch out for bob cats, raccoons and skunks at dusk, etc.) and then kicked off The Party with a toast to the three people for whom it was created. Not into public speaking and true to her nature, she kept it short. And she didn't exactly engage even Beth in the eye.

"I want to thank you all for coming to celebrate the lives of these three members of our family, each in a milestone year: Stefani Michel, 16, Maria Wyman, 70, and Jock Wyman, 80. Individually they are milestones, and collectively, they add up to 166 years of experience on this planet.

"You honor them by your presence, each one of you. There are 119 beings here tonight, including Misty the beagle and Mesmer the cat, who love this trio.

"Today we celebrate Youth, Beauty, Age, Wisdom, Family, Love and Friendship. May your world be rich with each.

"Oh, and, there will be Clogging Lessons later to songs like *Honky Tonk* and *Honey I'm Good*, so just remember:

step rock step,

step shuffle step,

step rock shuffle step.

Have a good time."

Jock Toasts Himself

Jock really loved those tasty little Margaritas, and by the time he stood up in his place at the table to toast himself, Maria and Stevie, Maria had cut him off. "You're too old to get drunk, Jockie," she whispered, and filled his glass with water. He scowled at her, but he didn't mean it. He felt no pain, but he wasn't drunk.

He stood up and tapped his glass with a spoon for attention.

Jock's gravelly voice didn't have much volume. Felix handed him the mic from the set of Tate & the Old Boys.

"This has been a quiet year for me, personally, as my children and their children and men and friends confront their dramatic lives. I am 80, so I may say, in public and without shame, that I have set aside many worldly things, in order to better confront and, indeed, embrace old age.

"My Maria tells me I am maudlin about this exploration at times, and I should just get on with it, not ponder so much. Perhaps she is right. Old age compensates for youth by its very release of what Kierkegaard and Sartre and their brethren referred to as existential angst. I'll leave that to the next generations. I'll ask Stevie to write about it, Tate to sing it, Jolene to paint it.

"With what years I have to walk this earth, I shall do so with my Maria, traveling the globe. We have recently returned from Alaska, where we fished for salmon, cooked it over an open fire and hiked in the wilderness. Expect to hear from us next from Fiji, where we will dance with the natives, drink kava kava and eat grilled fish someone else cooked. More on that as we develop our plan.

"And what, you may ask, will happen to Sweet Farm? I can with confidence tell you that the farm is in good hands, and I'm proud of the team my family has become. I love being an emeritus. My daughters, Rita, Nana and Fox, have grown into fine and curious women, and their daughters, our Tate, Stevie and Jo, make me proud. Everybody's so danged interesting. Really. No one is ever bored here. I can't tell you how happy that makes this old man. We came here to build a home for our family and, well, here we are, 24 years later. Mighty fine. It's mighty fine.

"Well, with the support of Fáno, Deke and the Rodriguez family, the women here on Sweet Farm, who are the real leaders, you know, they hold all the knowledge, and the history and, they have skills. I see nothing but blue fields ahead.

"Of course Maria will want to be in the Lavandula studio between jaunts around the world, so you will not be bereft of our company for long.

"But I say this: Seize the Day. Take it by the horns. Life speeds by like a race car."

A little before 7:00 Beth gathered up her charge and pushed the bamboo wheelchair back along the path to Nana's room in the Adobe House where Mrs. Cooper planned to rest.

Mrs. Cooper slipped right into dreamland and soon was breathing in and out and in and out in quiet bliss. Beth could still feel the pulse of the party. She covered the old lady with the soft cotton blanket and tiptoed out the door.

Beth followed the path from Nana's room back down to party central by the Barn. Just as she entered the trumpet vine zone, Fox came her way.

Fox surveyed her creation: The Party. She felt its pulse, too, and it was good. Tate would be singing soon, so Fox started up the path to the Adobe to get Jock and Maria, resting in their room.

She listened to Two Guitars and an Autoharp while moving along the vine-shrouded path. Sweet kids, and, out of tune. Fox wanted to share the moment with Beth—they would laugh about what it took to tune an autoharp.

Fox thought about Beth as she turned the corner toward the house, into the thick trumpet vines. She wished her clippers were in her pocket. She lifted the vine back with her right hand to see if she could tuck it out of the way. Just as her hand lifted the vines, Beth's beautiful little face appeared. She looked like a wood nymph: white blonde hair sparkling with current, straight bangs touching her brow like fringe, like soft feathers, like down. Around her neck a small single diamond dangled on a chain. Fox had never noticed it before. Next to the diamond was a tiny mole. Inexplicably, she wanted to touch it.

Beth watched her toes along the path. She had tripped over an exposed root on the way up to the Adobe and now checked for the spot. When Fox pulled back the curtain of thick green vines and red flowers, the scent overpowered Beth's olfactory senses and threw her right to Tahiti, her favorite spot on earth. She looked up. She wanted to be there, in Tahiti, with Fox, in bikinis, on the beach, lying on giant bath towels, glistening with oil all over their skin, reading out loud, perhaps the letters of Anaïs Nin.

The two women looked at each other for a full minute, both lost in fantasies of how they would like to spend the rest of their lives with this person. They each thought, *How do I tell her?*

Beth had never seen Fox's eyebrows move so close together, tiny tracks of worry. She reached out her hand and touched those tiny tracks. It was the lightest touch, like a whisper, a breath. It barely grazed Fox's skin, but it felt like fire.

In that moment, their eyes knew each other for who they really were. They drew closer, each small movement sealing their fate.

Fox knew. Beth knew, for sure.

What comes after?

That little kiss lasted three hours. Ok, three seconds, but in those three seconds, at least two lives were changed forever. A few more lives would change, too, in the inevitable domino effect of love.

Beth kissed with relief, exhaling all the unsaid words of love she kept close to her chest these months. She murmured in Fox's electric hair, she whispered in her ear, she breathed love dust into the air and surrounded them with it, covered them with it, enveloped them for eternity with the sheer power of her relief.

Fox kissed with surprise, with glee, feeling as if she had been an unbaked pie and this kiss was the heat and fire that would finally bake her into perfect doneness. She breathed in the scent of Trumpet flowers mixed with the civety smell of Beth's skin. She knew she never wanted to be any other place than in Beth's arms. Her heart was beating double time, but she was calm. That was it in a nutshell. She got it. She was flipped out in one way, but completely calm inside. As if…as if she knew all along, had seen, but had not believed, until this moment.

They broke apart as Jock and Maria appeared on the path. "We were just coming to get you," Fox said with a smile. She squeezed Beth's hand and let it go. "Tate's about to sing."

No one noticed Deke Harley, stepping back into the shadows.

Deke Harley

The sheer number of people made Deke want to hide, and, amidst the noise and the high spirits, he didn't know if he wanted to laugh or cry. He wanted to be alone. His pipe, pouch and a handful of Strike Anywheres were in his pocket. The lavender fields called to him. So, he went to the fields for a smoke.

As far as parties go, it was a success. Deke was glad for that. Personally, he felt empty. Things weren't going his way. Oh, Tate was terrific, and the family was so good, and good to him. And his mom was here and that was nice. But his main reason for coming back to Sweet Farm, to be with Fox, was never going to happen. He could see that now. She went through the motions. But those motions were not driving her toward him. He didn't know what she wanted, wasn't sure she knew what she wanted, but it became more obvious every day that she didn't want him.

His usual return path to the Barn was filled with tables and chairs, so he wandered around the loop in the driveway to cut across the garden. As he stepped into the loop, he saw Fox and Beth meet on the path by the trumpet vine. He saw Fox move the vines; Beth appear. He saw them look at each other, and he could swear he heard their thoughts. He heard them say I love you, although they didn't speak. He saw them bend toward each other, he saw them kiss, just for a moment. And he was pretty sure he saw sparks fly.

Tate and Farley

Tate, on the stage with her guitar, stepped into her natural place. She sang two of her own songs with such heartfelt meaning, such poise and, indeed, showmanship, she caused many a tear in the eyes of her audience. She closed her eyes and sang to her father, like she used to, only now, he was there, and she could open her eyes and see him and sing to him for real. She decided to look every single person in the audience in the eye, and sing to them, too.

She invited Farley up to join them, glad of his company. The Old Boys stepped back with the pan pipes and harmonica to make room for the big handsome college boy, come home to sing for his friend. Farley's dark hair was slicked back with Brylcreem. His white shirt and red tie gave him away as the big handsome college boy.

Farley leaned into the microphone and crooned, "I wrote this for you, Stevie."

Just as he began to sing, "Let's be friends, let's start over, let's go back to four leaf clovers," practiced with Tate over the phone, he glanced up to smile at Stevie, and saw her kissing a perfect stranger.

Well, not *the* Perfect Stranger. That was surely over. But, who was *this* guy? Who was *this* kissing his Stevie?

Farley's mouth went dry. Tate saw where his gaze fell. She had seen this coming. OK.

"Farley," she whispered. The friendly, family-filled and expectant audience waited. His father the judge, as well as Mrs. Simpson and Farley's sister, Karen. Henry Pedigo, soon to ship out to Vietnam, was there with Karen's friend, Pammie Stewart. About 100 pairs of eyes were focused on Farley Simpson at that very moment.

"Farley!" Tate whispered, louder. He snapped his head around, like he was coming out of a bad dream. He looked terrible, like he just received the worst news, which he had. She looked him in the eye. "Sing it, Farley. Sing it, now." And she strummed the cords and sang with him. She sang a clear harmony. She stayed with Farley, as any true blue friend would when seeing his heart break in pieces before her eyes, in fact, before the world.

What an odd moment for Tate: nervous as a cat on a sizzling Arizona highway, unsure of anything, any of this. She worried all day about being good enough, about not being flat, about being flat chested, about That Night, about everything. She got into her groove though and, then focused on Farley, who could never have sung that song without her in a million years. *I love you enough to be your friend, it'll keep us together, in the end." Geez.*

Farley was so grateful he wanted kiss Tate's feet, but in the middle of a hurt so deep, he could only nod at her and escape the stage. Oh, he waited until that lie of a song was over, until the audience applauded his mournful broken-hearted tenor beauty, until he was sure that they were applauding him and had not seen the flutter of the wind through the trees when the lips of his rival, whoever he was, whispered across the upturned mouth of his, Farley's girl.

The Old Boys played *Norwegian Wood* so Tate could gracefully leave the stage. When out of the light, she chased after Farley and grabbed him by the shirtsleeve. He turned around, a combination of sadness and fury turning his face into a mask. His cheekbones shone with bright red spots. The fiery tears in his eyes turned to ice. The lines in his face, usually indicating a smile, turned down, arrows of the deepest sorrow.

Tate started to speak, not knowing what to say, but Farley put up his hand and said, "Don't. I don't want to know. It doesn't matter." And he turned away.

Deke & Farley

Deke was sitting on the low fence by the Barn when Farley stopped and asked for a light. Deke handed him a Strike Anywhere match which Farley struck on a nail in the fence. He lit a Winston and blew out the match.

Farley asked Deke, "What do you do when the woman you want doesn't want you?"

At first Deke thought Farley was talking about Fox and Beth, Perhaps Farley had seen them, too, maybe everyone saw them…then he realized Farley meant Stevie, Farley's Stevie.

Judging by the body language, she's not Farley's, not by a long shot.

Farley followed Deke's eyes. Where the garden meets the lavender field, where the light dims and the scent increases, the two young almost-lovers stood by an arbor of pink Cecil Bruner Roses. They looked as one, those two, standing there starkly outlined in moon shadow. They melded together, he held her in the curve of his body, they fit together like two spoons. Deke thought, like Fox and Beth.

Farley turned away. It was all he could do to keep from throwing up. He took three deep breaths. He dragged on his cigarette and turned to go.

Deke reached out to say, "Stay," but the look on Farley's face told a story Deke could not take in right now, could not fit into his head, considering his own sad tale.

Hey. At least Stevie was kissing a man.

Peter Monk

The inside of Peter Monk's head was brimming with creative thoughts. He was so full, he could feel his brain expanding against his skull. He felt as if he could conquer the world.

He held in his arms the key to his future. He had at his fingertips the life of lives—two women, an almost born heir (a son of course), an island in the Pacific with his name on it (Monk's Landing), the gift of gab, the knack of convincing, the ability to manipulate energy, and enough weed and coke to create a fortune and stay high as a kite forever.

However, he could get into trouble dallying with a sixteen year old, obviously a virgin, so he watched his Ps and Qs with his young protégé. His plans were bigger than immediate gratification. He could get that anywhere. In fact, he had a date in about an hour for some immediate gratification.

Besides, there were pounds of pot to protect from the cops. He looked over his shoulder enough as it was.

Stevie was no dummy, but currently her common sense was clouded by passion. He teased her just enough to keep her interested. Another one of his manipulating traits. "Always leave them wanting more."

Peter didn't give a fig for Farley Simpson. This was no contest. Farley Simpson didn't stand a chance.

 Stevie's Little Red Book

Wow.

Chapter Nine

The End is the Beginning

Fox never had so much fun in her life. Everyone one danced. They were all on the rolled-out dance floor, clogging away with complete abandon.

Step rock step
Step shuffle step
Step rock shuffle step

Even the two year old Mabel stomped her tiny feet and waved her little arms more or less in sync with the music and the other dancers. Betsy carried her baby on her back. Fáno and Rita danced side by side in perfect step, laughing, like they'd been clogging for years.

The Ridge Boys' enthusiasm got people moving so fast they knocked over a stage light. But the dancers kept on, another hour went by and, after much hilarity and stomping and hooting and hollering, the Party began to wind down.

Stevie and Peter Monk wandered off to the lavender fields. Farley was long gone, home to Salinas to tend his bleeding heart. Deke, too, was mysteriously absent. Jock and Maria went to the Adobe and everyone else found his or her own bed.

Fox said goodnight to the last guests at 11, paid the departing band and went toward her room. She passed a fully dressed and pretending-to-be-asleep Deke on the couch. She knew he was pretending and for once, she didn't care. She peeked through Tate's open door and saw her daughter reading in bed. They smiled at each other, nodded and actually blew kisses.

Fox went into her room alone. She took off her clothes, put on flannel pajamas and climbed between the sheets.

She sat quietly in the bed, mind on the many pieces of the evening's puzzle. She picked up her notebook, the only way she could keep it all straight, and jotted down a few notes for the next day: pick up Grand Mamá before the breakfast, write check to caterer, return beer keg. Then, Fox let her mind wander, let her consciousness stream through her production of The Party. It made her happy. Fox was happy.

What a success. A great party. Fox ticked off all the big and small successes of the day, quickly, so she could think about other things.

Tate! On target! What a natural performer. You'd never know it in her personal life. She's so shy. Wonder where she gets that? I'll have to ask her later about the little kerfuffle with Farley, but his song was beautiful, too, meant for Stevie, of course, who was otherwise engaged. Yeah, the kerfuffle had something to do with that.

The Ridge Boys knew all the right songs and got everybody going. That was a blast. What a good idea.

The food—perfect, right down to Rita's Trio Birthday Cake (layers of chocolate, vanilla and cherry covered in pink fondant and pink and red roses). *So sweet. What a work of art. Mmmmmmm. I wonder if there is any cake left in the cooler.* She got up and put her slippers on.

270

To her knowledge, no one got drunk or boisterous or inappropriate.

Jock and Maria were happy. Nana and Will, like teenagers.

Stevie…newly preoccupied.

Jo spent the entire evening with her grandmother, in deep conversation. Something to do with the danged key and the leather book.

And Becca Harley! She knew how to clog! She taught the judge and Doc Swain and Fox saw her pay particular attention to Pat Lovell's father, Max, visiting from Mobile, Alabama. He towered above her like a tree over a lily.

And Pat! Big Pat on that little stage with Tate & the Old Boys, in uniform, no less, and belting out *Amor ti Vieta!* She could see his song soaring over Saddle Mountain like a thing, a trajectory of sound on tenor wings into the Los Padres, stirring up all the wildlife and ruffling all the feathers in the forest.

Nothing went wrong. Absolutely nothing. At least in Fox's estimation. Beth went to bed early, but Fox understood. If she could have, after the moment she'll always remember as the Vines, she'd have gone to bed, too. Just to savor it, undisturbed.

In Fox's mind, everything on the planet was perfection. Her eyes were open like never before, like someone tapped her on the shoulder and took off her dark glasses and said, "See?"

The blue in her quilt was bluer, the stars in the sky brighter, the empty place in the center of her being…well, it was no longer empty.

She started laughing. She walked into the tent and opened the cooler. While she ate pink cake with her fingers, she thought about her life. She laughed and laughed.

Oh my God. There's nothing wrong with me, she thought, looking at a handful of pink cake. *I'm just in love!*

Epilogue

Call it fate, call it love, call it whatever you want, Fox found her true mate of all time on the night of The Party. It was written all over their faces, Fox's and Beth's. Tate pondered the changes in her mother. Beth went about her day and her job and her life on the other side of Carmel Valley Road in a state of pure wonder. Fox's hair sizzled in that red-headed way usually spelling disaster. This time was different. The coppery essence was holographic, shot through with rainbows of color, bending with the light.

"Good morning!" she said to Deke when she breezed into the office. Deke looked up. Fox's usually translucent skin was lit from within, glowing with a murmuring red. The fine fox hairs on her arms were electromagnetically charged, she felt alive and awake and surging with a palpable joy.

Deke knew, of course. As far as he could tell, he was the only one who knew. Fox had no idea he had seen her and Beth pressed together in the trumpet vines that night. "Dang it," he mumbled to himself. "Another burden to carry. Another danged secret." Perhaps something else to drop into his imaginary box in his imaginary closet of private knowledge and personal affairs. He wasn't sure what else to do with this information.

And Stevie! About to embark on a new and exciting chapter! We'll follow her in *See Ya, Foxie,* Book Four in the Lavandula Series, where she discovers that love's complexities are greater, and perhaps more disturbing, than even *her* imagination could conjure.

Recipes
from the
Sweet Farm Kitchen

Soup of Consolation

Buttermilk Muffins

Popovers

World's Greatest Pancakes

Roasted Chicken

Legendary Cream Scones

Lemon Curd

Soup of Consolation

Fáno sooths the family angst with Soup of Consolation.
It is his answer to everything from the common cold to
tears, tummy upsets to tummy butterflies.
Fáno's not-so-secret recipe

Roasted Chicken
10 cups assorted vegetables, rough cut: carrots, celery,
onions, garlic, potatoes, yams
3 tablespoons butter
2 cloves garlic
8 cups Clear Chicken Stock, see page 49
Pinch each: tarragon, oregano, thyme
Salt and pepper to taste
Herbs of love, spice of affection

In a large soup or stock pot, sauté vegetables in butter
and garlic.

Add one cup of the stock.

Using hand blender, grind vegetables with stock to make
a smooth paste. Slowly add the rest of the stock and
herbs. Simmer about fifteen minutes.

Serve warm with finely shredded chicken and Star Crou-
tons.

Buttermilk Muffins

```
12 ounce cup muffin pan
Baking spray

2                   eggs
2 cups              dark brown sugar
2/3 cup             canola oil
1 tablespoon        vanilla

2 cups              flour
1 tablespoon        baking powder
1/2 teaspoon        salt

1 cup               buttermilk
```

Preheat oven to 300°. Blend first four ingredients in Kitchenaid or other mixer. Combine four, baking soda and salt and add to egg mixture, alternating with buttermilk. Pour into muffin cups. Sprinkle with Muffin Topping. Bake about 30 minutes.

This batter can also be made into individual bundt cakes. In this case, sprinkle muffin topping into pan, add half the batter, more topping and the rest of the batter. Turn upside down after cooling.

Fruit variations: Add 2 cups peeled and chopped green apples, or one cup dried fruit hydrated in hot water and drained.

Popovers

375°

Popover pan or heavy muffin tin
or even a cake pan for one large popover called Yorkshire
Pudding
Vegetable spray

6	eggs
1 tablespoon	vanilla
1/2 teaspoon	salt
1 3/4 cups	flour
2 1/4 cups	milk (can be whole, 2% or fat free)
4 tablespoons	butter, melted

Blend eggs, vanilla and salt in food processor. Add flour
and milk alternately while food processor is whirling
around. Add melted butter. Pour into pitcher. Cover. Best
if refrigerated over night to cure batter (the popovers will
rise higher and pop better).

Heat popover pan or heavy muffin tin in oven for
about fifteen minutes. Quickly remove from oven, spray
heavily and pour cold batter to top of cups. Bake at 375°
(without opening the oven door) for about 40 minutes,
until dark golden brown and firm to the touch. Remove
from oven and, using bamboo skewer, poke with many
holes to allow the steam to escape (otherwise your
popovers will collapse). Serve with butter and jam or maple butter (1/2 softened butter, 1/2 maple syrup blended in
food processor).

Don't double the recipe. If you want more popovers,
make the batter twice.

The World's Greatest Pancakes

3 eggs
2 cups Fl our (all purpose, sifted)
2 1/2 cups buttermilk
1/2 Teaspoon salt
1 heaping teaspoon baking powder
1 teaspoon baking soda
1 tablespoon melted butter
1 tablespoon warm syrup

About an hour ahead of time, separate the whites of the eggs from the yolk. Let whites come to room temperature. Return yolks to fridge.

Preheat griddle to 400° (don't grease griddle).

When ready to proceed, put buttermilk in mixing bowl and add the soda. Stir. Put flour in another bowl and add the salt and baking powder. Beat yolks and stir thoroughly into the buttermilk mixture. Stir in the dry ingredients. Stir thoroughly – don't beat. Add butter and syrup. Stir, don't beat.

When griddle is ready, beat egg whites until they form soft peaks, then fold whites into rest of mixture. Using a cooking spoon, drop spoonsful of the batter onto the dry griddle, spreading lightly until each pancake is a little larger than a silver dollar (the old kind). Bake until air holes pop open and remain open. Turn once. Serve golden brown. Makes approximately 40 two-inch pancakes.

" Note: Serve on warm plates with warm syrup and butter. For a special taste treat, try strawberries and sour cream instead of syrup (these of course should be cold).

These pancakes should practically float off the griddle.

Roasted Chicken

Chicken
Oil
Salt
Herbs
Juice
Lemon or onion

Rinse a fat chicken thoroughly in cold water. Pat dry and let stand at room temperature for about an hour.

Pre-heat oven to 350°

Place dry, room temperature chicken in a sprayed or oiled ceramic or metal roasting pan (not glass – it splatters grease all over the place) and drizzle with olive oil. Rub it into the skin with your fingers. Rinse your fingers.

Sprinkle chicken with salt and herbs (unless it is a brined chicken – then, skip the salt).

Pour ½ cup orange or apple or grape or pomegranate juice into the roasting pan and stick a washed lemon or a whole unpeeled onion (with the ends cut off) into the cavity. Cover the chicken with a foil tent. Roast (it's really poaching at this point) for one hour. Remove the foil tent and baste the chicken every 30 minutes for another two hours. The chicken will get all lovely browned and crusty.

When you remove the chicken from the oven, pour off the juices/jelly into a bowl for later use in the soup you made from the stock you made from the chicken you roasted.

Legendary Cream Scones

350°

3 1/2 cups	pastry flour
3 1/2 teaspoons	baking powder
1/2 teaspoon	salt
1 tablespoon	bakers' superfine sugar

2 sticks (1 cup) unsalted butter, cut in pieces

4	eggs
2/3 cup	heavy cream
2/3 cup	sour cream

Sift dry ingredients. Beat eggs, cream and sour cream together in a separate bowl. Place dry ingredients and cold butter in food processor and process until mixture looks and feels like coarse meal, less than a minute. Add egg and cream mixture and flavor; quickly mix together until dough forms a soft ball. Scoop out about one cup of dough for each scone onto sheet pan covered with parchment. Sprinkle with sugar (optional). Bake about 20 minutes, or until golden and cooked through.

flavor possibilities:
1 cup dried cranberries (any dried fruit), hydrated in warm water for five minutes and drained or
1 cup raisins with 1 teaspoon cinnamon or
1 teaspoon lemon zest with 1 tablespoon lemon juice or
1 cup chopped crystallized ginger or
1 cup cheddar cheese, 1/2 cup parmesan cheese, 1 table-spoon each: dried basil, dried thyme, dried oregano (sprin-kle with parmesan instead of sugar)

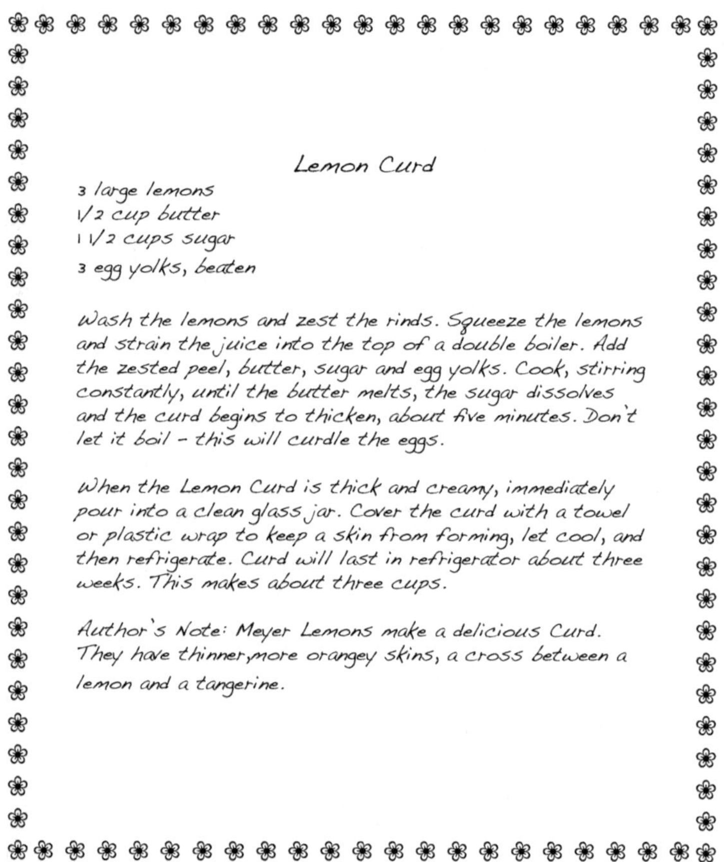

Lemon Curd

3 large lemons
1/2 cup butter
1 1/2 cups sugar
3 egg yolks, beaten

Wash the lemons and zest the rinds. Squeeze the lemons and strain the juice into the top of a double boiler. Add the zested peel, butter, sugar and egg yolks. Cook, stirring constantly, until the butter melts, the sugar dissolves and the curd begins to thicken, about five minutes. Don't let it boil – this will curdle the eggs.

When the Lemon Curd is thick and creamy, immediately pour into a clean glass jar. Cover the curd with a towel or plastic wrap to keep a skin from forming, let cool, and then refrigerate. Curd will last in refrigerator about three weeks. This makes about three cups.

Author's Note: Meyer Lemons make a delicious Curd. They have thinner, more orangey skins, a cross between a lemon and a tangerine.

Lavandula Series Drawings
by the author:

Bird's Eye View of Sweet Farm

Barn Front Elevation

Chapel House Front Elevation

Barn Interior

Chapel House Interior

Adobe House Front Elevation

Adobe House Interior

Sweet Farm Bird's Eye View

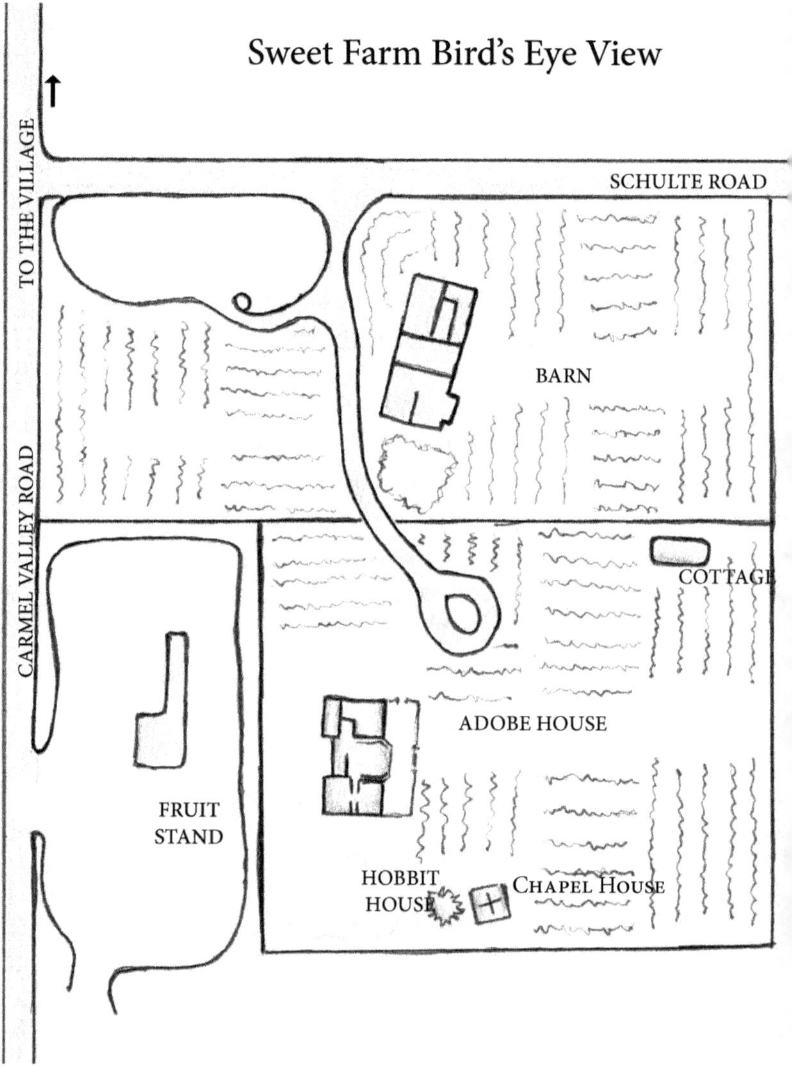

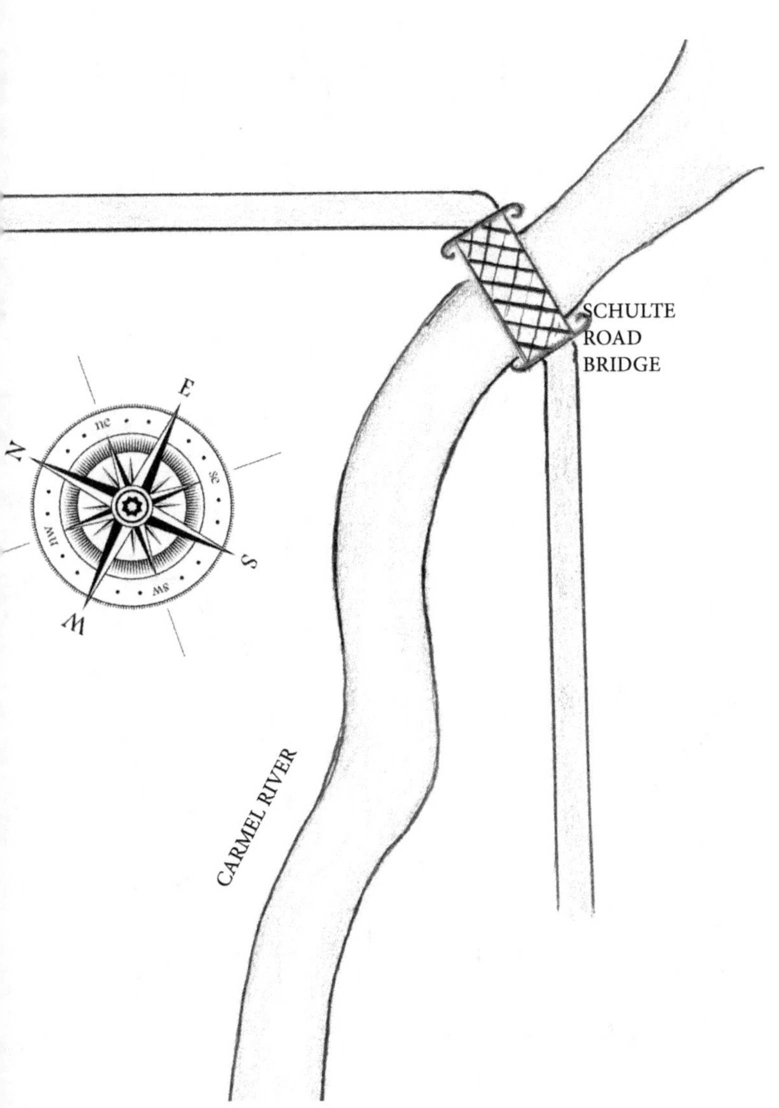

E
nc
N
se
NW
S
W
SW
CARMEL RIVER
SCHULTE
ROAD
BRIDGE

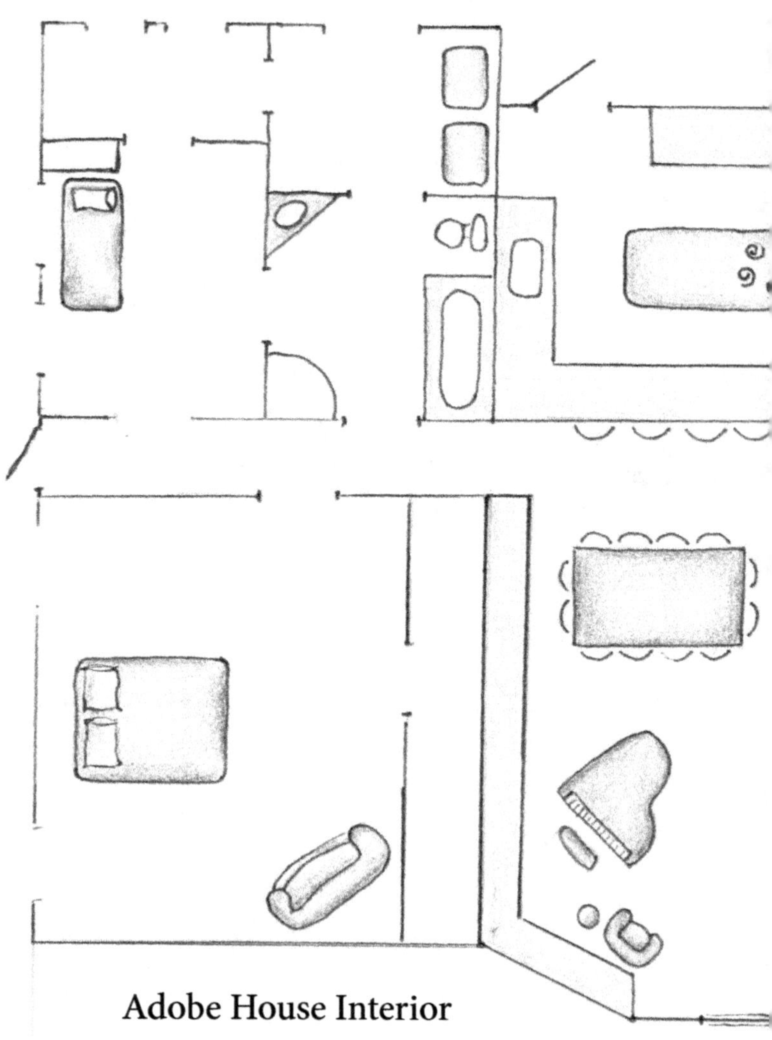

Adobe House Interior

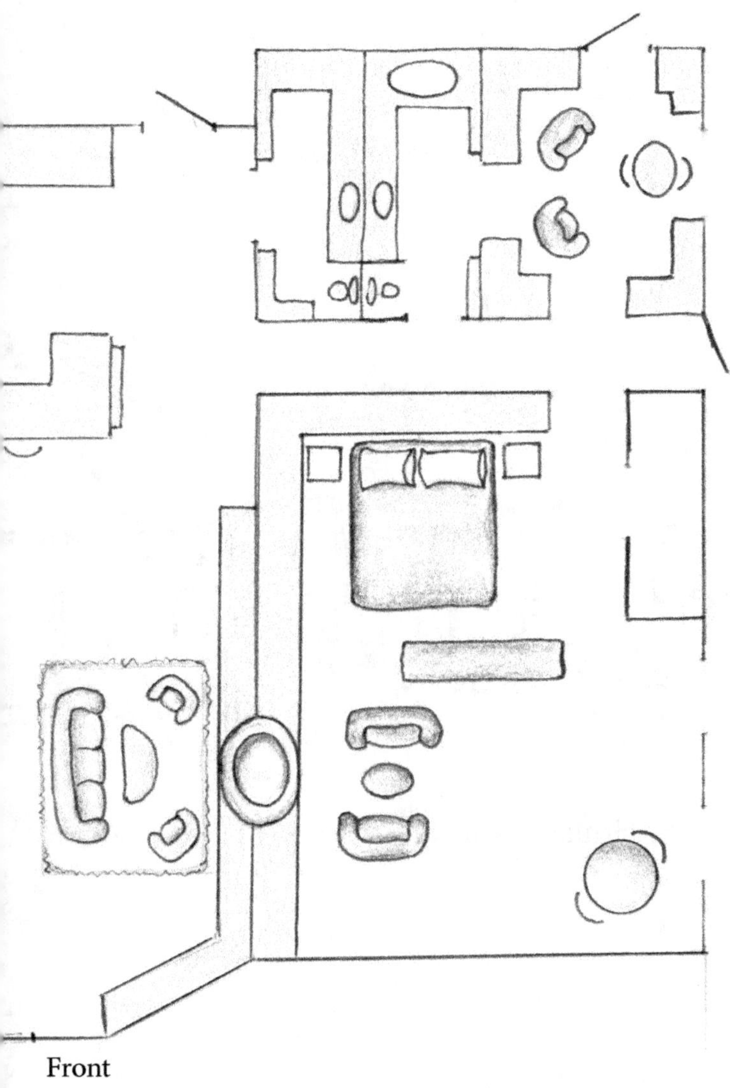

Front

Adobe House Front Elevation

Barn Front Elevation

Chapel House
Front Elevation

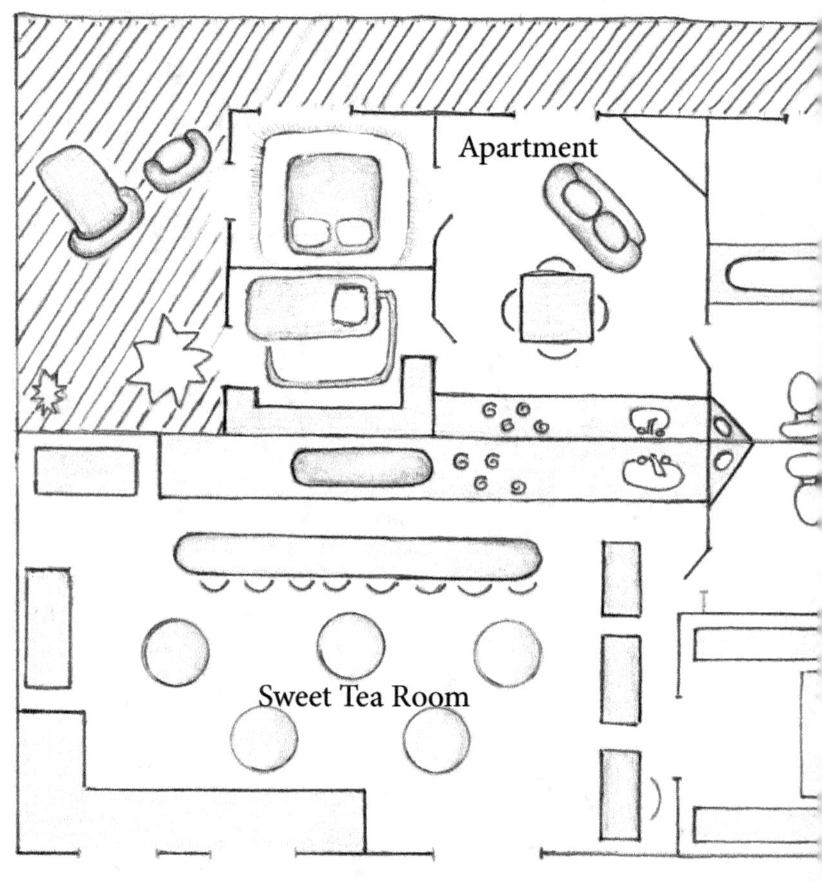

Barn Interior

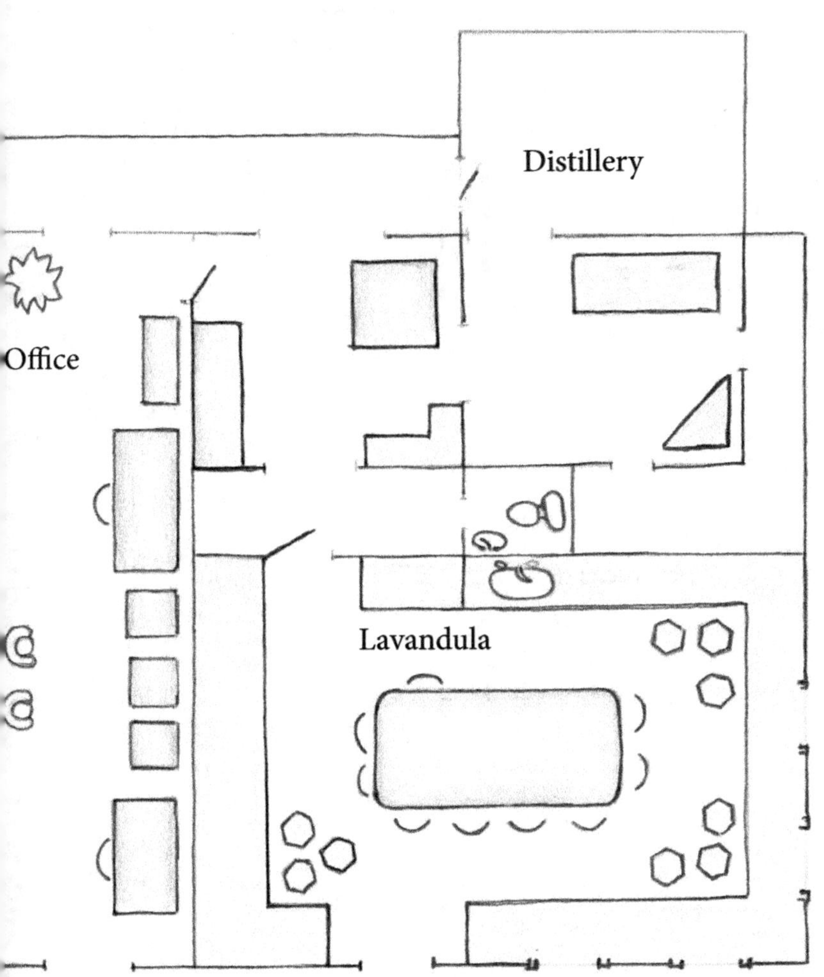

Distillery
Office
Lavandula

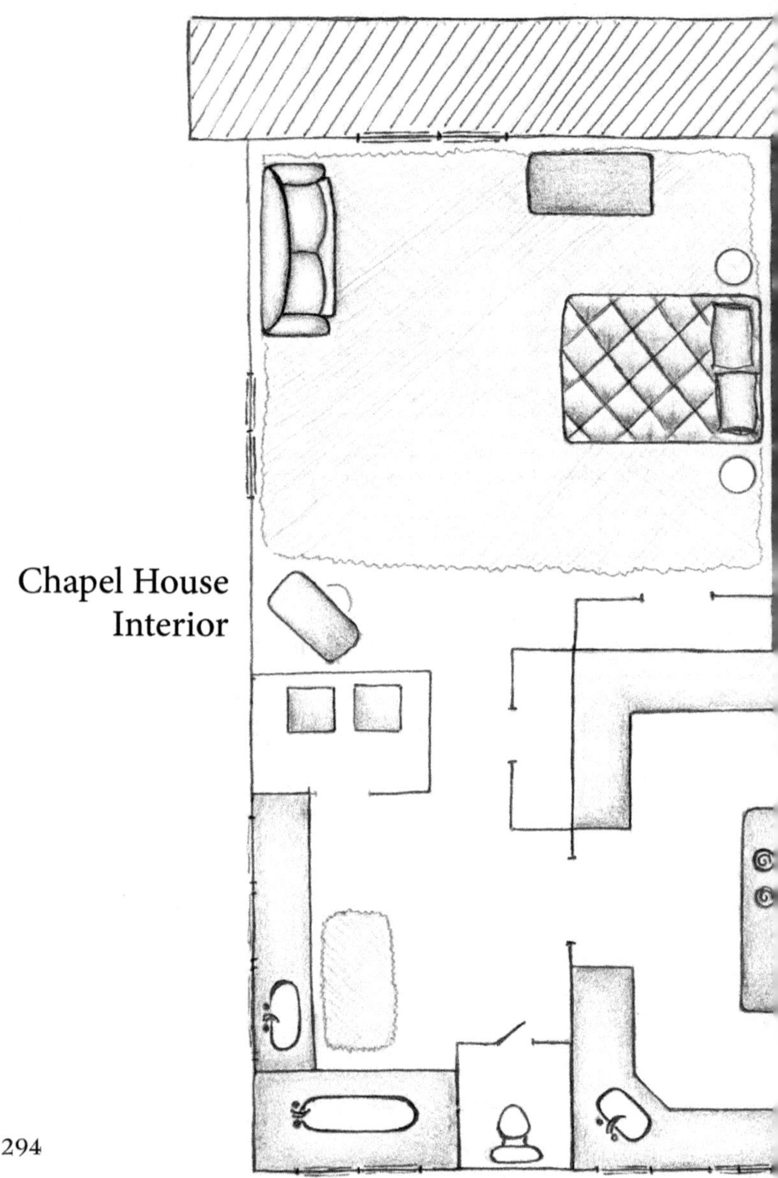

Chapel House
Interior

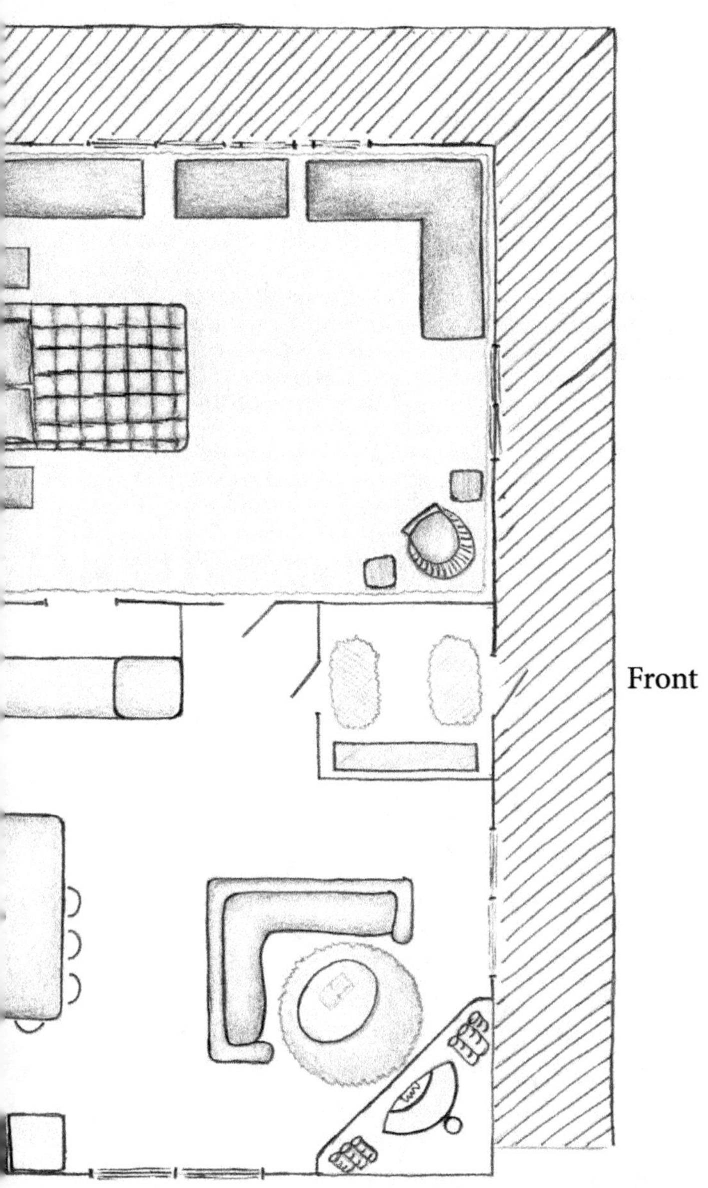
Front

Acknowledgements

It's all about relationships. Without relationships, nothing gets done. Collaboration, interdependence, inclusion equals more than the sum of our parts. The early readers of Humming in Spanish are this author's heroes:

Gates McKibbin - Thank you for moral, spiritual, edible and grammatical support, and for the insights about staying on the story's path.

Katherine Edison - Thank you for multiple readings, close scrutiny, minor suggestions and major solutions.

Gail Lindus (1947-2020) - I miss you every day. Thank you for reading out loud to George, loving my stories and characters and listening patiently to many iterations of a sentence.

Dr. Frank DeLuca - Thank you, not only for early reading and brilliant ideas, but for knowledge and understanding of the Enneagram, which gives my characters' personalities solid ground.

Anne Brooke Hawkins - You inspire me every day. Thank you for wrapping your arms around the Wymans and their shenanigans.

Carolyn Kingsnorth - Thank you for your insights and thoughtful comments. Invaluable, every one.

Pegge Goertzen Bragg - Thank you for your devotion to Sweet Farm and to me, your sister of a different mother.

David Gordon - You are the light that shines on my creations. "Thank you" hardly covers it.

The Lavandula Series
Based on the fictional journals
of Stefani Michel

Book One: *Looking for John Steinbeck*

Book Two: *Deke Interrupted*

Book Three: *Humming in Spanish*

Designed and produced by Lucky Valley Press
Jacksonville, Oregon www.luckyvalleypress.com

All images in this book © 2017-2021 by the artists

Stay tuned for further

developments in the Wyman story

in

See Ya, Foxie

Book Four in *The Lavandula Series.*

www.ingramcontent.com/pod-product-compliance
Lightning Source LLC
Chambersburg PA
CBHW070539120726
47909CB00007B/2182